DANGEROUS AFFAIR

Feisty Eve Masters has had enough of the rat race. A successful career in London has allowed her to retire at forty-three and move to Crete. There, she falls for the handsome, but quiet, David Baker — but despite the mutual attraction, theirs is a volatile relationship. However, this is not the only thing to keep Eve occupied. The day she arrives, an English ex-pat estate agent is found murdered. Eve is intent on solving the crime — putting her own life in danger . . .

IRENA NIESLONY

DANGEROUS AFFAIR

Complete and Unabridged

LINFORD
Leicester

First published in Great Britain

First Linford Edition
published 2013

A catalogue record for this book is available
from the British Library.

ISBN 978–1–4448–1758–4

Published by
F. A. Thorpe (Publishing)
Anstey, Leicestershire

Set by Words & Graphics Ltd.
Anstey, Leicestershire
Printed and bound in Great Britain by
T. J. International Ltd., Padstow, Cornwall

This book is printed on acid-free paper

1

John Phillips sat back in his armchair, sighed deeply and took a sip of whisky. As the warm peaty liquid slid down his throat, he became oblivious to the tiresome shouting of the other person in the room.

John cared little what other people thought of him. He wasn't a popular man, and was used to having abuse hurled at him. However, his business was successful and he had a healthy bank account, so what did it matter at the end of the day?

Putting down his glass, John picked up a cigar. He ran it appreciatively under his nose, savouring the bouquet and smiling with satisfaction, then took out his lighter. He wished his visitor would leave so that he could relax and enjoy his whisky and cigar in peace.

Although just fifty-two, John was

already starting to show the tell-tale signs of good living. His stomach overhung his belt and he often seemed out of breath. His doctor had diagnosed both high blood pressure and high cholesterol, but unfortunately John was reluctant to take any steps to lower either.

However, he was tall, his eyes were a clear, deep blue and his dark brown wavy hair had not a hint of grey. If only he didn't drink so much or overeat, he could still be thought of as a very handsome man.

It had been a good day for John. He was an estate agent on the island of Crete, Greece, and he also organised the building of new properties. Despite the current recession, today he had succeeded in selling two houses.

However, he had unfortunately fallen behind schedule on completing a new home for one of his clients, Eve Masters. She was arriving from England the following day, so he thought it the best tactic to keep a low profile. She was definitely a tough cookie, and he could only imagine her reaction on discovering that her dream property was in less than perfect, move-in condition.

The other annoyance was that his unwanted guest would just not shut up.

Finally, John decided that he'd had enough of the tirade, so he turned round to say something to his visitor. However, as he looked up, he saw something decidedly unexpected — his ornamental miniature statue of Aphrodite, the Greek goddess of love, bearing down towards him.

He tried to both move and shout at the same time, but everything happened so quickly that his glass went flying across the room and his cigar fell to the floor just before Aphrodite connected heavily and sickeningly with his head.

The last thing John Phillips saw was the furious expression on his visitor's face relaxing into a broad smile.

2

The hot air enveloped Eve as she got off the plane. It was early August in what was turning out to be a particularly hot summer in Greece. Some of the passengers were fanning themselves with their passports and complaining, but Eve was smiling. She thought of the rain she had left behind in England, and how everyone back home would be jealous.

'Isn't it wonderful?' Eve remarked to a man standing next to her. 'I can't wait to get to the beach.'

'It's a bit too hot for me,' he replied, wiping his forehead with his handkerchief.

Eve turned away, not wanting to let anyone spoil the first day of her new life on Crete. What did the man expect in Greece in August?

Half an hour later she was in a taxi,

driving towards her new home. She had come in February to search for property and had chosen a house that was one of John Phillips' new projects.

It had just been a shell at the time, but it was perfectly situated at the edge of a village within walking distance of a couple of shops and tavernas. It had beautiful views of both the sea and the White Mountains, and Eve was excited to see the finished product.

This was a new beginning and she couldn't wait to see what the future held, but although she knew that Crete was the largest of the Greek islands, she hadn't given much thought to the possibility that there might not be enough to occupy her. She was used to the hectic atmosphere of London, and she loved the pace of life there. Would she be happy without the theatres, art galleries and upmarket restaurants she was so used to?

The taxi suddenly overtook on a blind bend and Eve sat up abruptly.

'Hey there, be careful,' she shouted at the driver.

He merely grunted in response.

'Probably doesn't understand a word of English,' Eve murmured to herself. She chose not to acknowledge the fact that she herself hadn't bothered to pick up more than a few words of Greek and had little intention of learning the language.

Eve settled back in her seat and closed her eyes, thinking it would probably feel safer if she didn't see what was going on.

* * *

Eve Masters was forty-three years old and had made enough money to give up her job, having been a successful showbiz agent in London. She had decided to move to Crete, the most southerly of the Greek islands.

An attractive and petite woman, with blonde hair and green eyes, Eve's body was perfectly toned and she always wore smart and expensive clothes. However, her outward appearance concealed a slightly overbearing personality. She could be bossy, found it surprisingly easy to alienate people, and although she considered herself to be popular, most of the people in her social circle were business colleagues.

Eve had never been married, and while men were initially attracted to her, they were often put off by her assertiveness. Unfortunately, she didn't realise it was her fault and went into each relationship with the same attitude.

However, Eve did have a soft side and if she were given the chance, it would surface. A difficult childhood with parents who cared more about their careers than her had made her wary of people in general, but deep down she desperately wanted to be liked. She just didn't know the right way to go about it.

The taxi screeched to a halt and Eve looked out of the window. The wall looked half finished and the garden was a mess. The taxi driver hauled her luggage out of the boot and didn't seem at all happy when she didn't give him a tip.

Eve silently reminded herself that it might be a good idea to learn more about local customs and expectations before she got much further. She shrugged, opened the front door and wandered into the house, flicking on a light switch.

'At least the electricity works and the furniture is all here,' she said out loud, 'but I'm not happy about the state of the garden, not happy at all.'

Eve returned to the front door for her luggage then went and unpacked. Most of her things were coming with a removal firm, but she had brought her personal essentials. She had also asked for some basic furniture to be put in the house to tide her over until her own arrived. She decided that a good soak in the bath would help calm her down before confronting John.

I don't believe it, she thought when she entered the bathroom. *They've not finished tiling! I'm going to have a lot to say to that John Phillips tonight. I can't abide shoddy workmanship. He's got another think coming if he imagines that he can take me for a ride!*

At least the solar panel was working and Eve could relax in a warm bath. Closing her eyes, she suddenly felt homesick.

★ ★ ★

An hour later Eve walked into the local bar, The Black Cat, feeling refreshed, all thoughts of England having faded away.

It was still warm and she had put on a tight-fitting sleeveless turquoise dress, being both slim and fit enough for it to look stunning. Eve had gone to the gym regularly in the UK, realising that now she was in her forties, nature would take over if she didn't do something to counteract it.

She was pleased she'd gone to a

tanning salon a few times before coming to Crete. Eve knew she looked good with some colour, and although she occasionally thought about the risks to her skin and vowed to keep out of both the sun and the salons, the resolution never lasted long. She hated being pale, and looking around The Black Cat, it seemed as if the majority of people had also put the adverse effects of the sun to the back of their minds.

The bar was about ten minutes walk from Eve's new home, in the next village and situated right next to the sea. It was a regular haunt of the British ex-pats and was run by Ken and Jan Stewart, a couple in their mid-thirties who had moved to Crete from their native London four years previously. Ken was short and chubby, with blond spiky hair, while Jan was lanky and towered several inches above him. They had been married for six years, and despite the light-hearted banter they often exchanged while working, they seemed to still be very much in love.

Eve couldn't spot John Phillips anywhere and thought he was probably avoiding her, knowing that she was arriving on Crete today. Then she saw Laura James, her holiday rep from the year before, sitting with her Greek boyfriend, Yiannis Neonaki.

Laura was in her mid twenties and was small and pretty, with fair hair and big blue eyes. Eve noticed that Laura seemed quiet and sad, while Yiannis was ignoring her and having a loud conversation with people at the opposite end of the bar. Eve wondered whether she should have a word with Laura about her house. After all, when she had professed an interest in buying property, Laura had recommended John. As she approached her, Eve thought she saw Laura wipe away a tear.

Eve felt uneasy. Laura had changed since they had first met, and Eve felt sure this was due to Yiannis. Eve didn't like him. He was loud and didn't seem to respect women. The previous summer Laura had been a happy and fun-loving girl, but she had started going out with Yiannis during the winter, and when Eve had visited Crete in February she had already noticed a difference in her. Laura had been miserable, and once or twice Eve had seen her crying.

Eve had a bad feeling about her relationship with Yiannis and decided she would talk to Laura on her own when the opportunity arose. Eve thought of herself as an intuitive person, always having had the ability to recognise star quality in her clients back in England.

Her thoughts were interrupted when she spotted Annie Davies chatting to David Baker. She felt her heart rate quicken and immediately forgot about both her house and Laura.

Eve had initially met both Annie and David in February. Annie had moved to Crete with her husband, Pete, two years previously. He had been a police officer and she a teacher in England. They were both in their mid-fifties and Eve found them a very likeable couple, although she felt Annie could make more of an effort with her appearance. Annie was tall and slim, but she didn't bother much with make-up or with styling her hair.

Eve remembered the first time she had met David. She had been sitting in the bar wondering whether her days really could revolve around village life. However, just as she had been about to get up to return to her hotel, David had walked into the bar. He was stunningly handsome, at least six feet tall with jet-black hair and piercing blue eyes.

'Wow! Who's that?' Eve had asked Annie, suddenly coming back to life.

'That's David Baker,' Annie had replied, smiling. 'He's an actor, although he doesn't work much now. Occasionally he goes back to England for small TV parts, but recently he's been concentrating on writing a novel.'

'Is he married?' Eve had asked Annie.

Smiling again, Annie had formed the distinct impression that Eve wouldn't hesitate in going after anything or anyone she wanted.

'Divorced,' Annie had replied. 'I don't think the marriage ended well. His wife had an affair and he was terribly hurt. I think it's made him wary of women.'

Although nothing had happened between Eve and David in February, she had thought of him many times in the past six months. She was delighted that he was in the bar on the first night of her new life back on Crete.

'How wonderful to see you again, David!' Eve gushed, kissing him on the cheek and sitting in the chair next to him.

Annie grinned, thinking how little Eve had changed.

'It really is good to be back. I've missed you all,' Eve said.

David was feeling uncomfortable, finding it impossible to think clearly when Eve was around. She had gone through his mind many times in the past few months, but his feelings had always been mixed. Sometimes he thought of how brusque and bossy she could be, but then he thought of those cat-like eyes of hers and the smile that lit up her face.

He had imagined taking long walks with her along the beach and kissing her under the stars. The stars were spectacular on Crete because there was hardly any light pollution, and after a hard day writing, David would often sit alone on his balcony, gazing at the sky.

Recently, realising that Eve would soon be returning to Crete permanently, he had found her creeping into his mind more often. However, he told himself he didn't need any distractions. He'd been getting on well with his novel; it was almost finished.

Suddenly, the door burst open and Betty Jones rushed into the bar, looking distressed. Everybody turned to look at her and David was relieved that Eve's attention was taken from him.

Eve groaned when she saw Betty. The two women had taken an instant dislike to each other when they had first met six months earlier. Betty and her husband, Don, were both in their sixties and had lived on Crete for many years. Betty had formed a drinking group in The Black Cat, and Eve had heard that she liked to take charge of the British community in the village. Eve had decided that Betty was manipulative and bossy.

'Here, come and sit down,' Annie said. 'What's happened? You look terrible.'

'You haven't heard? John Phillips has been murdered!'

'What?' Annie exclaimed. 'But that's impossible — I only saw him yesterday!'

'One of his builders went to his house this morning and found him dead,' Betty continued, trembling. 'He'd been hit on the head and the house ransacked. His money box had been forced open and the police seem

16

to have decided that it was a robbery gone wrong. From what I've heard, they're not taking that much interest. As you know, a few houses have been broken into lately and they haven't arrested anyone.'

'Typical,' Eve grumbled. 'I bet if it was a Greek that had been murdered, they'd be on the job straight away.'

David sighed, wondering why Eve had moved to Greece. She didn't seem to have a high opinion of either the people or of their way of life.

'I'll get you a drink, Betty,' he said. 'G and T?'

'Thank you. Make it a large one, please.'

David grinned, knowing that all Greek measures were large. Sometimes you could end up with more gin than tonic!

'I don't suppose I'll ever get my wall and garden finished now, then, shall I?' Eve sighed.

Annie was shocked at how selfish Eve could seem in such circumstances, but she acknowledged that many other people would also now be worried about their homes being completed.

'I'm sure there'll be lots of other people stuck with unfinished houses too,' Betty broke in, voicing Annie's thoughts.

'Really?' Eve asked, becoming intrigued.

'Even Don and I had problems with him. I don't know why we didn't keep the first house we bought here, I really don't. Instead we were stupid enough to have a house built through John's property business,' Betty continued. 'He kept charging us more than he quoted to complete the house, and if we didn't pay up, work stopped. There are still things waiting to be done, even now. And you, Annie — your patio still isn't finished, is it?'

'No, but I'm sure it was on his list.'

Eve remembered that Annie had been constantly making excuses for John back in February.

'You're too nice, Annie,' Betty admonished her. 'You need to toughen up a bit or people will walk all over you.'

Annie didn't bother to reply, knowing that once Betty started ranting, she stopped listening to anyone else.

'Mind you, what with all the problems John's caused, there won't be many tears shed over his death, I can tell you,' Betty continued, getting into her stride.

Ironically, Eve was starting to feel alive. She had been having decidedly mixed feelings about moving to Crete. While the possibility of getting to know David better excited her, she had begun to worry that village life might be too dull — but at the moment it was nothing of the sort.

'You know that John made a pass at Laura a few days ago?' Betty dropped her voice, hoping that Laura and Yiannis wouldn't hear her. 'She turned him down flat, obviously, but as you can imagine, Yiannis wasn't too happy about it. There was almost a fight in here.

'And then John owed Ken quite a lot

of money. He kept putting off paying his tab, making all sorts of excuses. No — there won't be many people who are sorry he's gone.'

'My goodness,' Eve remarked. 'If we were in an Agatha Christie novel, there'd be a long list of suspects.'

'Yes, and you would be one of them,' Betty quipped before the seriousness of the situation overcame her and, breaking into sudden sobs, she rushed off towards the Ladies.

'Oh dear, I'd better go and see if she's okay,' Annie said, rising to her feet. 'I don't know what brought on the tears. She's probably worried about getting her house finished.'

'I was still in England last night, so how could I have killed him?' Eve demanded crossly, turning to David. She paused for a moment, thinking, and then smiled broadly, a brilliant idea suddenly coming to her. She grabbed David's arm and stared excitedly into his eyes.

'This is all very interesting, isn't it?'

she murmured, raising her elegant eyebrows. 'I'm sure there's more to this than the police think. How do you fancy a bit of amateur sleuthing?'

'I think that might be a bit risky, don't you?' answered David hastily. 'I'm pretty sure it was only burglars — but if it turned out that it wasn't, then we could end up in trouble. I'd hate for you to get hurt.'

Eve thought David must care about her to be worried for her safety, but she didn't think of thanking him and hurried on, carried away with her idea.

'Oh come on, David — I can tell that you enjoy a bit of adventure. It would be fun. After all, there's not much else to do here, is there?'

As Eve turned to talk to Pete, David shook his head. He still couldn't fathom why Eve had made the decision to come and live on Crete. She seemed bored already, and he couldn't understand why she had stopped working at such a young age. Although money evidently wasn't an issue, it was obvious that she did need excitement.

Crete was ideal for people who wanted a quiet existence, but this wouldn't suit Eve, he mused. She was a passionate and complicated womanwho needed to live a full life. He also wasn't convinced that she would be able to embrace the Greek way of life. It was very different to English customs, and David didn't think she had the patience to try and understand it. He found himself fascinated by Eve's beauty and energy, but unfortunately she was taking his mind off his work and he wished he could stop thinking about her.

'What do you reckon, David?' Her persuasive voice echoed in his ear.

'Eh? Sorry — I was just thinking about John,' David lied.

He knew Eve wouldn't like it if she knew he hadn't been giving her his undivided attention.

'We're going to Annie and Pete's for a drink and a chat. It'll be quieter there.'

'Sorry, I can't. I have to go home and get on with my writing. Only a few more chapters of my novel to go.'

With that remark, David got up and left, feeling out of his depth with both the murder and with Eve's arrival. Whenever things got too much for him, he just wanted to be alone.

Eve was stunned by David's abrupt departure. How rude he was, going home without even saying goodbye! She'd been expecting him to be delighted to see her again after so long, and she was more disappointed than she liked to admit by his apparent coolness.

Perhaps he wasn't worth bothering about, after all. Well, she wasn't the type of woman to chase after a man — and if David wanted her, he would have to come and find her!

3

The following morning David was surprised to hear the doorbell ring. Looking down from his upstairs balcony, he saw it was Eve. He suddenly felt hot and bothered.

'Come on, let me in. We need to talk,' she shouted up.

Eve had tried to put the events of the previous evening to the back of her mind, but had failed miserably and lain in bed fuming for half the night.

Why hadn't David come along to Pete and Annie's? She found it difficut to believe that he hadn't wanted to spend the evening with her, and in a fit of pique she had decided never to speak to him again!

However, this was all forgotten by the morning and she had awoken visualising his sky-blue eyes gazing lovingly into hers. She imagined him sliding his arms around her and kissing her passionately. Eve thought how fit he looked for a man approaching fifty, and was impressed that, like her, he hadn't let himself go. She had decided they suited each other perfectly and determined to go over and speak to him.

Reluctantly David came down the stairs, with an awful feeling that Eve was planning something with regard to the murder. Since he'd been up late writing, all he wanted to do was lie in the sun and relax. The novel was coming on well and he needed to put all his energies into finishing it — not divert them into a complicated relationship. Or a murder enquiry.

Still, Eve did look particularly gorgeous today.

'You really should have come to Annie's last night,' she said without preamble. 'We had a good chat about the murder. Well, most of us did. I don't know why Phyllis was there. She just sat in the corner and said nothing.'

'Give her a break,' David answered

sharply. 'It's not long since her husband, Len, died. It's difficult for her, especially being left alone in a foreign country. He was only diagnosed with cancer after they moved here, but they'd sold everything in England, so she has nothing to go back to. You know how difficult it is to sell property here, with the Greek economy being what it is.'

Phyllis Baldwin was a small, plain, quiet woman who was in her mid-fifties. She had moved to Crete with her husband early the previous year, but he had died around Christmas.

Eve found Phyllis unutterably dull, never having had much patience with timid people, but she felt a pang of guilt when David explained about Len.

Nevertheless, she countered tartly, 'Well, I'm alone here and it doesn't worry me. And from what I've heard, Betty does everything for her now, so Phyllis doesn't have to deal with anything too difficult.'

'But you chose to come here on your

own — she didn't,' David pointed out. 'Anyway, you're a much stronger person than she is. I imagine that you could cope with anything.'

That was putting it mildly, David added silently, and wondered why he felt the need to constantly make excuses for Eve's behaviour. He looked at her, standing poised and graceful in his hallway, and wondered whether his feelings for her were based purely on her physical appearance. She didn't seem to be a compassionate person — but he supposed she could be hiding her true personality behind an assertive front.

Eve, meanwhile, was taking what David had said as a compliment; she prided herself on her strength of character and appreciated it when others saw it. She preened slightly.

'Going back to yesterday, how was Betty later on?' David asked, deciding that it was better to change the subject.

' I have no idea. She went home quite soon after you left and didn't come to

Annie's.' Eve paused for a moment and then quickly continued, 'Listen — you and I need to talk about the murder. The police think it was a burglary, but I'm pretty sure that someone John knew murdered him. Nobody seemed to like him. Don, Betty, Pete, Annie, Yiannis, Ken — they all have a motive, and I'm sure lots of other people would have liked to have seen him dead, too.'

David shook his head. 'I hardly think an unfinished house is motive for murder, Eve — and anyway, no one would ever get their money back if they killed John.'

'Well, it might not have been premeditated,' Eve offered. 'Whoever did it could just have gone over to John's house to confront him and then got carried away. I find it hard to believe that it was Pete or Annie as they're such lovely people, but I wouldn't put anything past Betty.'

'Oh, come on, Eve! Betty might be a bit unpleasant at times, but I can't see her murdering anyone.'

'Well, what about Yiannis? I hear he was very angry when John made a pass at Laura. These Greeks can be very unpredictable, you know.'

'You amaze me, Eve!' David snapped, his temper rising. 'If you dislike Greeks so much, why on earth did you come and live here? They're a wonderfully warm race of people and have been nothing but friendly to me.'

Eve grunted. Things weren't going as well with David as she'd hoped. She decided she'd better keep any further negative opinions to herself and endeavoured to think of something nicer to say, but before she could speak, they heard barking just outside the front door.

'Probably another of those stray dogs.' David sighed. 'I'll go and shoo it away.'

Eve followed him and smiled as he opened the door.

'Oh, it's that lovely dog again. She was hanging around my house this morning,' she said. 'She must have followed me here. Looks as if she needs a home.'

'A lot of animals here need homes, Eve. It's not like England. There are so many strays wandering the streets, you can't help them all.'

'Well, I could help one, don't you think?'

David shut the door on the dog, mystified. Eve had shown little sympathy for John or Phyllis, yet she wanted to care for a stray dog. She was definitely a complicated character — and David hoped that it meant she wasn't as completely heartless as she sometimes appeared to be.

Just as they turned away from the door, there was a knock, and David, with Eve still standing beside him, opened it.

'I thought I saw you come in here,' a voice boomed. 'How dare you accuse me of murdering John!'

'I did nothing of the sort, Betty!' Eve replied, amazed at the accusation coming out of the blue.

'Well, you certainly implied it at Annie's. Phyllis told me everything you said. What makes *you* a detective?'

For once, Eve was lost for words. She knew she hadn't once said that she thought Betty had killed John.

'I'd appreciate it if you kept your nose out of my business, thank you!' Betty snapped, glaring at Eve and, turning on her heel, she left as quickly as she had arrived.

'Well!' Eve gasped, completely affronted. 'That was strange, to say the least.'

'I hate to ask it, but did you say anything about Betty murdering John last night, Eve? Even something that might have simply implied that you thought she might . . . ?'

'No, I did not!' Eve was quite upset that David could even think that she would openly accuse anyone of murder. 'All I said was that John was causing problems for Betty and Don by not completing their house. I didn't say at any time during the evening that I thought Betty had killed John! I know I sometimes speak without thinking, but I'm not malicious.'

Eve was close to tears and David found himself wanting to put his arms around her. He stopped himself. She looked so sad, but he had been hurt by his wife and had vowed never to rush into a relationship again.

Still, he was growing to like the new side he was seeing of Eve's personality; she had surprised him by showing her vulnerability. He had imagined she was the type of woman who didn't care what other people thought, but it looked as if he was wrong and she wasn't as tough as she seemed.

Nevertheless, he remained cautious; he intended to take things slowly with Eve, and hoped she would accept the situation.

'Oh, enough talk about the murder,' Eve said, pulling herself together. 'I have a vivid imagination and you're probably right that this was just a robbery. Perhaps I should write a novel as well! Tell you what, how about lunch? My shout.'

David didn't think for one minute that Eve had put aside all thoughts of solving the murder, but perhaps a long lunch would allow him to get to know her better. He didn't think that would be moving too fast.

'Okay — why not?' he replied. 'Where do you fancy?'

'I've heard that Hari's is excellent and that they do really good vegetarian food.'

David was pleasantly surprised again — one of his own foibles was always imagining vegetarians as kind and gentle people. There seemed to be so many contradictions to Eve, but whatever her story was, at this moment all he wanted to do was spend more time with her.

4

Hari's was only a ten-minute walk away and they decided to go on foot, as David felt like having wine with his lunch and they would also be given complimentary tsikoudia, or raki as the locals called it, at the end of the meal.

Raki, the local firewater, was an acquired taste, but Eve had already decided she liked it. Although she had some negative feelings about Greece, she thought the Cretan custom of free raki, and fruit or cake, at the end of a meal, was very pleasant.

Temperatures were forecast to reach thirty-eight degrees today, and as much as Eve loved the heat, she was worried that a walk in the sun might mess up her make-up. She hadn't bought a car yet and had been hoping that David would suggest taking his.

As he shut the door, the dog rushed towards them and Eve bent down to stroke her, thinking how much like a wolf she looked. However, the animal didn't seem at all fierce and Eve felt she was just looking for a good home. When Eve straightened up, David had already set off walking down the road and she had to run to catch up with him. There was no opportunity now to suggest taking the car.

In the end, though, she enjoyed the walk. She quickly forgot about the miserable taxi driver who had brought her this way from the airport. Although the land was dry and she wasn't able to see the beautiful wild flowers that had been around in February, the hillsides were covered in olive trees and the valleys filled with orange and lemon groves.

When they arrived at Hari's, there were people sitting in the sheltered area outside. The taverna was next to the beach, and with a pleasant breeze coming off the sea and the air-conditioning not being switched on, it was more comfortable outside than in.

David noticed Pete and Annie at one of the outdoor tables and was disappointed. If they ended up chatting to them, the conversation would no doubt lead to the murder and he didn't want to talk about it. However, he knew Eve was keen to solve the crime, and while he was aware that she was attracted to him, he also knew that she was a highly intelligent woman who needed more stimulation in her life than just romance.

He imagined she could easily become frustrated, especially living on a Greek island; he wondered how she would cope during the winter when all the tourists had left and most places in the resorts had shut down. Chania, the nearest major town, stayed busy during the winter, but it certainly didn't have the buzz of London.

Eve headed straight for a vacant table close to Pete and Annie, and David sighed. His vision of a romantic lunch with Eve was fading. Why couldn't she forget about the murder for a few hours and concentrate on enjoying a good meal and conversation with him? David wasn't that interested in who had killed John. He hadn't liked him, that was certain, but he felt strongly that it was a matter for the police — not for amateur sleuths.

He would have been even more upset had he been aware that Eve had chosen Hari's precisely because she had known Pete and Annie would be there, and she was hoping to discuss the murder further.

They sat down and looked at the menu.

'From what I'd heard, I thought there'd be a better choice for vegetarians than this.' Eve sounded cross.

David felt confused again. At home, he had started to think that Eve was a much kinder person than she had first seemed, but now she was complaining again.

'Would you like to go somewhere

else?' he asked, attempting to sound polite.

'We're here now, so we might as well stay.' Eve grunted. 'I suppose I can just have a selection of starters. Melitzanosalata sounds okay — that's an aubergine dip, isn't it?'

David nodded in reply.

'Then I can have fried mushrooms and a village salad. Oh, they've got baked feta as well. I like that,' Eve continued, sensing that David was disappointed in her behaviour. 'And you always get fresh bread and olive oil, so that should be ample.'

David didn't know what to think now. On the one hand, Eve seemed to be making an effort — but he couldn't help wondering whether she had only agreed to stay in the taverna to talk to the others about John.

Eve, on the other hand, was annoyed with herself. Things had started to go well between her and David, but she knew she had acted childishly over the menu.

David hoped that Eve might relax once the wine came, but just as he started to fill her glass, she noticed Ken and Jan walking towards Hari's. She quickly turned towards David.

'Pete said last night that John's tab at The Black Cat had reached at least five hundred euros,' she whispered. 'Don't you think that's motive enough for murder? After all, John's money box was forced open and all the cash was taken.'

'I've known Ken and Jan since they moved here and they're a great couple,' David retorted angrily. 'I can't even imagine Ken murdering anyone.'

'Well, perhaps it wasn't premeditated.' Eve repeated her previous theory, not put off by David's tone. 'He could have gone over to ask for his money, got into an argument and then hit John on the head on the spur of the moment He probably didn't mean to kill him.'

'Be quiet,' David hissed, as Ken and Jan sat down at a table close to them.

However, David wasn't surprised when Eve turned and spoke to them. 'Not open today, then?' she asked them.

'Not until six on a Monday,' Ken replied. 'We've found that it's the quietest day of the week.'

'Well, everyone needs a break,' Eve conceded. 'You can't work all the time.'

She was unaware that Greeks worked seven days a week during the season to earn enough money to get them through the winter. It wasn't easy to get a job when the tourists had left, and the work that was available, such as olive or orange-picking, wasn't well paid.

Eve decided that having got Ken's attention, it was an ideal opportunity to talk about John. 'Terrible business about John Phillips. I hear he owed you money, Ken. I doubt if you'll ever see that again.'

'A couple of hundred euros,' Ken replied with a shrug. 'I suppose I'll have to write it off. Makes me a bit wary of giving people tabs from now on, though.'

As David's eyes met Eve's, he knew what she was thinking.

'Well, somebody's lying about the amount,' she whispered urgently in his ear.

'Be quiet,' David said sharply under his breath. 'I've heard people say John owed Ken all sorts of different amounts — that's what happens *when people gossip*,' he added pointedly.

At last Eve was silenced. She knew David was irritated with her and she was mortified. She so wanted to form a relationship with him . . . but solving the murder excited her as well. Why couldn't she have both?

Once the food arrived, Eve finally started to relax. She asked David about his previous career and his face lit up when he reminisced about acting, telling her how much he missed it, but that he had never been able to get the big break he had hoped for. He was delighted that Eve genuinely seemed interested in what he had done, and it was good to talk to someone who knew about show business.

However, just as David was starting to think the day had taken a turn for the better, his heart sank as Betty walked into the taverna. Betty and Don lived almost opposite Hari's and David suspected that she had been looking out from her balcony watching what was going on in the taverna.

'Have you heard the latest?' Betty asked Annie, speaking loudly enough for everyone to hear. 'The police have been questioning John's workmen. Apparently, he owed them a few weeks' wages and I reckon the police suspect that it was one of them who killed him.'

Eve stared at her. It made sense, but it wasn't earth-shattering. She was hoping the murderer was one of the ex-pats, feeling that it would be much more newsworthy. If she managed to prove that the killer was one of the British, she would probably end up on the international news, which would be wonderful!

'Oh, you're here,' Betty remarked

sarcastically, looking at Eve casually as if she'd only just noticed her.

Eve was brought back down to earth. Why was Betty so loud, and why did she have to turn up again?

'Hopefully not spreading any more nasty rumours about me,' Betty continued, glaring at Eve.

'That's enough, Betty,' David broke in. 'Eve told you she wasn't accusing you of murdering John, and that should be an end to it.'

Betty started to say something, but then decided against it. She considered David a real gentleman and didn't wish to turn him against her.

'Why don't you join us for a glass of wine, Betty?' Annie invited her. 'Hopefully the police will sort this out soon and we can all get back to normality.'

'But can we?' Eve interjected. 'Some of our houses are still unfinished. What's going to happen about them? Most of us have paid in advance for work that hasn't been done. The business was John's, so who'll take over, and will the work ever get finished? Does anybody know anything?'

Eve was getting worked up. She had no financial problems and could afford to have the work finished by someone else, but she didn't like being conned.

'I'm sure his estate will cover everything,' Annie soothed.

Annie always looked on the bright side and thought the best of people. Eve half wished she could be like her, but experience had taught her that this was a naïve attitude.

'Let's hope there's enough money left to cover all his debts,' Ken observed.

'I doubt it,' Betty chipped in. 'For once I agree with Eve. I don't think the outlook is promising. I reckon they'll try and make us pay again to get our homes finished.'

Everybody fell silent.

'Come on,' Pete said. 'There's no point worrying about things until they happen. All we can do is wait and see what the police come up with. Let's order more wine and talk about something else. Come on, Ken and Jan, come and join us.'

They pushed the tables together, Eve making sure that she was still sitting next to David. She decided to put all thoughts of the murder to the back of her mind for now, but she was determined to get to the bottom of it all.

She looked at David, thinking that he ought to be thoroughly impressed with her if she discovered who the real murderer was before the police did. She took a sip of wine and smiled, thinking that life was definitely good today.

5

Eve's mobile rang, waking her from a deep sleep. It was pitch dark, and for a brief moment she forgot where she was. Fumbling for the light switch, she glanced at the clock and was surprised to see that it was almost ten.

They had stayed at Hari's until after six, and Eve thought it was rather nice not to be rushed out of restaurants as you often were back in the UK. Here you could stay in a taverna all day without ordering anything else apart from your meal. When Eve had got home, she had sat outside for a while, but feeling her eyes closing, had decided to go upstairs and lie down.

'Hello,' she mumbled into the phone, wondering who could be ringing this late.

Eve was unable to see the caller ID. She hadn't admitted it to anyone yet, but her eyesight had started to deteriorate a little. She did have some reading glasses, but they were hidden away in a drawer. She only took them out occasionally and never, in front of other people.

'Hi, Eve, it's Annie. Are you okay? I'm really sorry if I've woken you.'

'Oh, don't worry about it, Annie,' Eve replied. 'I felt a bit tired and dozed off, that's all. Is anything wrong?'

'No. I just thought you'd be interested to know that the police are keeping Petros, John's foreman, in custody tonight. He says he was out with his cousin from Mykonos the evening John was killed, but they can't seem to find this relative of his. All the other workmen have solid alibis.'

'Oh,' Eve replied, trying not to sound disappointed. 'I wouldn't have thought Petros was the killer. He seems like such a nice guy, but I suppose you never can tell.'

'No, I wouldn't have thought it was him either, but you know Pete was in the police force and he says there's certainly no stereotype. Look — you sound tired, so I'll let you get back to bed. Speak to you soon.'

Annie hung up, thinking that Eve was probably not too happy that her days as an amateur sleuth could be over.

Eve put her mobile down and sighed. This wasn't the best end to what had been a lovely day. Her thoughts drifted back to lunch at Hari's.

After David had chastised her for thinking that Ken might be the murderer, she had avoided talking about John, not wanting to upset David any further. She had hoped to show him her nicer side and had even made an effort to be pleasant to Betty — though she definitely didn't like or trust her.

The day had ended surprisingly well when David gently kissed her as they had left the taverna. Unfortunately, Betty had already gone home, but everyone else had seen the kiss, and Eve hoped one of the others would tell her about it, knowing it would annoy her. Or perhaps Betty had been spying from her bedroom window! Eve had a feeling that she would not be Betty's first choice as a partner for David.

Eve and David had accepted a lift home from Annie and Pete. All four lived in the same village, and although Eve was fit, after indulging in plenty of food and wine at Hari's, she didn't feel like walking uphill in the heat.

Meandering up the road, they had approached Phyllis's home, which was in between the two villages. Eve had glanced at the house and noticed how perfect the garden was. Phyllis had managed to keep the lawn alive, despite the months without rain, and she had some beautiful roses.

At that moment Eve had thought she saw Laura going into the house, but knew immediately that she must be mistaken — why would those two would be socialising? Phyllis only seemed to be friendly with Betty, and Yiannis didn't like Laura having

English friends any more.

But after thinking about it, Eve had told herself that the girl could have been anyone; after all, she had only seen the back of her from the car.

* * *

Eve switched off her mobile after Annie's call. Even though it was only just after ten, her eyes were starting to close again and she didn't want to be disturbed for a second time that night.

As soon as her head touched the pillow, she fell asleep, but because she had slept during the evening, she didn't have a good night and kept waking up. In the end she got up at half past five, deciding that it was pointless lying in bed awake any longer.

She stayed at home all day in the hope that David would call round. After all, he had kissed her — even if it was only a light brush of the lips. However, the day dragged by and there was no sign of David and no phone call.

Although she wanted to see him, she was reluctant to go to his house. Despite giving the impression of being a very modern woman, Eve could be old-fashioned in some ways, too, and she believed that because he had kissed her, it was now up to him to make the next move.

But what if he was regretting the kiss and was now avoiding her? She had been imagining romantic walks and candlelit dinners with him. She didn't want these dreams to be shattered.

Eve didn't know what to do with her day. She was bored with sunbathing and wished she had a landline with an internet connection, but she had been told it would be a few weeks before it would be set up. She had given up her English iPhone and decided she would have to go into Chania and buy a Greek one, or perhaps a dongle for her laptop. She felt quite cut off without email and video calls.

* * *

The following morning, Eve sat on her patio, feeling low, the depressing thought of another day like the previous one occupying her mind. Her dreams of both a relationship with David and the excitement of solving the local murder had disappeared into nothingness.

She took another sip of coffee. It was yet another hot summer morning and she thought that in an ideal world it would have been perfect to go to the beach with her gorgeous neighbour and discuss strategies to solve the murder.

Her thoughts were interrupted by a knock at the door and she jumped up, hoping it was David. It was still early; perhaps he had come to ask her to join him on his morning walk. He had told her he enjoyed a stroll each day before he started writing.

Hurriedly she brushed her hair and went to open the door, but although she tried to smile, her visitor could tell immediately that she had been hoping it was someone else.

'Good morning,' Annie greeted her.

'You look tired.'

'I'm afraid that I didn't sleep well last night. I can't believe it, but the air conditioning packed up. I don't reckon it was a new unit at all. There seems to be one problem after the other with this house. That John has a lot to answer for.'

'Yes, you're right. Other people are complaining about the inferior work of his builders, and everyone's getting worried that the outstanding jobs won't get done. Even I'm starting to get concerned,' Annie said, an uncharacteristically worried look coming over her face. 'Anyway, the reason I came over was that I have some news. The police have released Petros. His cousin from Mykonos turned up and said he was with him on the night of John's murder. Apparently he'd gone to Gavdos, the little island to the south of Crete, and had forgotten to take the charger for his mobile — that's why they weren't able to contact him.'

'Really?' Eve exclaimed. 'I knew it! I

had a feeling Petros wasn't the one who murdered John. He's such a lovely man, and there are so many more likely suspects.'

'I hope you're not going to start accusing people again,' Annie said cautiously. 'Betty was very upset that you thought she'd killed John.'

'Of course I won't interfere.' Eve grunted. 'What could I do anyway? I'm not a detective. And anyway, I didn't accuse her. She doesn't like me at all, does she? I can't imagine why.' Eve paused. She hated it when people disliked her. 'Has Betty said anything to you about me?' she continued.

Annie knew that Betty was jealous of Eve, but she didn't want to inflate Eve's ego, or to cause any more problems between the two women. Things were already getting tense whenever they were together, and Annie had come to Crete for a quiet life, not to be a referee.

'I'm sorry, Eve,' she said now. 'Betty doesn't confide in me.'

Eve wasn't sure she believed her, but

she didn't have time to talk. This was the ideal opportunity to see David. Although she knew he wasn't keen on helping her search for the killer, she imagined she could convince him. However she didn't want Annie to know her plans. Let her think that she had put all thoughts of the crime out of her head.

As she bade her goodbye, Annie was certain Eve had no intention of forgetting about the murder, and suspected that she would soon be on her way to David's house to ask for his help. Annie felt a little guilty, thinking she shouldn't have told her that Petros had been released — but reassured herself that Eve would have found out soon enough anyway.

As soon as Annie had gone, Eve dashed upstairs to get ready. She didn't want David to think that she was making a great effort to impress him and so decided to dress casually, putting on a T-shirt and tailored shorts, knowing she still had good legs. Then she did her face. Eve always wore make-up, taking great care over it so that it never looked overdone.

She brushed her hair and secured it with hairspray, not wanting to look windswept when she arrived at David's. Although the temperatures were already in the mid-thirties, there was a hot southerly wind blowing. Eve had heard about the winds of Crete and she was already thoroughly fed up with them.

Finally, she glanced at herself in the mirror and smiled, knowing she looked good.

As Eve double-locked her front door, she remembered everyone talking about burglaries, and resolved to see about getting an alarm system fitted. Strolling out of the garden, she was pleased to see the stray dog coming towards her wagging her tail, but was concerned to see she was limping.

'Here, dog!' she called. 'What have you been up to?' Patting the animal, Eve looked carefully at her leg and examined it gently, but thankfully nothing seemed broken.

Having bought some dog food and a dog bed a couple of days previously in the hope that her canine visitor would return, Eve went back inside to get them and filled a bowl with water. After drinking and eating appreciatively, the dog sniffed interestedly at the bed positioned in the shadow of the wall, and then flopped on to it, evidently feeling at home already.

'Now, listen,' Eve said. 'I have to go out, but you lie there and rest your leg. Now, I can't keep calling you 'dog', can I?' Eve paused for a moment, reviewing a series of possible names, and then continued, 'Portia, that's what I'll call you! Anyway, I'll see you later.'

The dog looked at Eve, panting, and curled up in her basket. Portia had found a new home.

*   *   *

It only took Eve a few minutes to walk to David's house. She was excited about seeing him and started off quickly, but soon her steps slowed. It had been a long time since she had felt so attracted to a man, and she was unsure of how she should act. David's ex-wife had hurt him and he needed to be approached gently, but Eve wasn't used to being subtle. As she neared his house, she saw him sitting outside, reading, and stopped to observe him.

Suddenly she felt nervous, and wondered whether he would be pleased to see her. She had been thinking of him constantly since they had said their goodbyes at Hari's, but now she felt like turning back. Perhaps he really did wish he hadn't kissed her? But either way she had to know and, after a few minutes, she braced herself and went towards him.

'Hi there, haven't seen you for a while!' she said, smiling.

David looked up. Eve looked stunning, but he'd been unable to think clearly about her since their lunch. Once she had stopped talking about

John Phillips, she had been great company, and by the end of the meal the only thing he had wanted to do was kiss her — but once he had returned home, he wondered if he had done the right thing.

Although he had enjoyed being with Eve, he knew she could be hard work. Her mind needed constant stimulation, and he still wasn't sure whether he wanted the stress of a relationship with anyone at all — let alone her.

'Have you heard?' she asked. 'The police have released Petros. They've ruled him out as a suspect since his cousin from Mykonos turned up to give him an alibi.'

David's heart sank, knowing that Eve would now want to resume her search for the killer — and that she would inevitably want him to help. He didn't want to get involved in something that could potentially be dangerous, but she would probably get into trouble on her own and he didn't want that to happen.

And she did look utterly beautiful, so

perhaps it wouldn't be such a bad thing to spend more time with her . . .

'I suppose you're going to try and find out 'who dunnit' then?' he asked, not wanting to commit himself.

'Well, I don't really think the police know what they're doing, particularly when they're dealing with the English. I just thought I might make some discreet enquiries. Don't worry,' she added quickly, seeing David frown. 'I won't go rushing into things.'

'Have you given any thought as to who the likely suspects are?' David asked. He was slightly anxious about her response, knowing that there would probably be friends of his on her list.

'Well,' Eve replied, pausing. 'I don't think Pete and Annie are involved — or you, of course,' she added, laughing. 'I know that you like Ken, and personally, I don't *really* think he's capable of murder either, but you must admit he does have a motive. Yiannis is a prime suspect, of course. He does have a terrible temper and John did make a pass at his girlfriend. And then there's Betty . . . '

'*Betty?*' David interrupted. 'I know you don't like her, but I can't see her killing anyone! And anyway, what would she have to gain?'

'Again, it might not have been premeditated. She could have gone over to John's to ask when her house would be finished, they could have ended up arguing and then she could have hit him in the heat of the moment.'

David shook his head. 'Any other ideas?' he asked.

'No. Don is very mild-mannered — I doubt he's capable of being a murderer. Phyllis is quiet and didn't even have her house built by John. Can't see any motive there. Then there's Laura, but she's tiny and Yiannis hardly ever lets her out of his sight.'

Eve paused for a moment, and David could almost see her mind working overtime.

'I've had an idea,' she said excitedly. 'We need to get everybody together.

What about a housewarming party at my place? What do you think? People often say things they shouldn't when they've had a few drinks.'

David knew there would be no point trying to stop Eve — and in any case a drinks party didn't sound too risky, especially as he would be there to keep an eye on her.

'Okay,' he agreed. 'I don't know what you hope to gain out of it, but I suppose it won't do any harm.'

'Well, with two of us keeping our eyes and ears open, we might find out something. You never know — the murderer could be somebody we've not even thought of.'

'Possibly. I suppose it's worth a shot. When were you thinking of having this party, then?'

'No time like the present — how about Saturday night? You don't think too many people will be booked up already?'

'Not many people here have tight schedules, so I'm sure it'll be fine,'

David replied with a wry smile.

'Okay, then — I'd better dash home and start setting things in motion. You'll come over early to help get everything set up, won't you?'

David nodded resignedly. When Eve had hurried away, he sat back in his chair and closed his eyes, deciding to rest in the sun for a couple of hours before resuming his writing. He had a feeling that his quiet and peaceful life was over, and the next few days, if not weeks, would be decidedly hectic.

6

Eve didn't want to get up. It was only seven in the morning and she felt like rolling over and going back to sleep, but it was the day of the party and she had lots to do.

She wanted to impress David with her culinary skills, and had decided to have a buffet rather than just putting out nibbles. She wasn't the most innovative of cooks, but if she put her mind to it she could produce dishes that looked sophisticated, while not being too difficult to prepare. She wanted everybody — especially Betty — to think that she had taken all the time and trouble in the world preparing the food, even though she had no intention of spending hours in the kitchen.

Eve hadn't seen David since she had decided to throw the party, but he had promised to come over an hour early to help her get ready, and the thought of seeing him again spurred her into action. The party was going to start at six, and if she spent time cooking in the morning, she'd have plenty of time after lunch to get everything else ready.

★ ★ ★

'Damn!' Eve muttered angrily to herself a couple of hours later, not caring that Portia was the only one who could hear her and couldn't understand. 'This pastry really isn't turning out like it's supposed to.'

Portia, looked up at her from her bed, but seeing there was no food on offer, went back to sleep. Eve was struggling with mini quiches, but her cooking skills didn't extend to making good pastry. She decided to go to the village shop; despite being small, it stocked some quite unusual items, and she hoped that they might have frozen pastry. She was certain that nobody who would be at the party would be able to tell the difference.

Eve picked up her car keys. Feeling lost without her own transport, she had hired a car the day before. She needed to go to Chania to get an iPhone or dongle, and she had also thought of asking David to help her choose a car of her own. There were showrooms for most makes of cars in Chania and she quite fancied a sporty model.

It only took Eve a few minutes to get to the shop, and she was heading straight for the frozen section when she heard a familiar voice reverberate through the building.

'Good morning! Can't wait for the party later on.'

Eve was mortified to see Betty bearing down on her. The last thing she wanted was that woman seeing frozen pastry in her basket! Eve knew Betty would tell everyone, and was relieved that she hadn't picked up the pastry before Betty had approached her.

'Yes — look forward to seeing you

later on,' Eve lied, moving away from the frozen foods.

'It's so nice of you to invite us,' Betty replied.

Eve wasn't fooled by Betty's attempt at being gracious but decided to play her at her own game. 'Not at all. You've all made me feel so welcome that it's the least I can do to thank you.'

Despite her cheerful face, Eve was tensing up, knowing the minutes were ticking by. She wandered around the shop and picked up a few extra packets of crisps and nuts, thinking that you could never have enough food at a party anyway.

Glancing at her watch, Eve started to get irritated. Would she have enough time to get everything ready? The only thing she hadn't put in her basket was the pastry.

Finally, to Eve's relief, Betty went to the till and then left, shouting out a loud goodbye. Eve grabbed the pastry and quickly paid for everything. Time was getting on and she wanted everything to be perfect that evening.

* * *

David was punctual, arriving at five as arranged. He thought Eve looked particularly attractive this afternoon — not that he'd seen her looking anything but amazing. For such a handsome man, he had very little self-confidence and couldn't believe that this beautiful woman could be interested in him.

Eve was wearing a snug-fitting sleeveless yellow dress and David noticed how firm her arms were. He imagined she must work out to keep her body in such good shape.

Eve smelled David's aftershave. It was one of her favourites, and for a moment she wished they were going to spend the evening on their own. However, she had to solve the murder first — then David would be impressed at how clever she was and realise that she was the only woman for him.

'Are you going to let me in?' he asked, grinning.

Eve seemed miles away and David wondered what was going through her mind. He thought she was probably thinking about John and the murder, and he hoped she would be discreet this evening. If the killer was one of the people coming to the party, he or she could panic if Eve asked too many questions. Her life could be put in danger — and despite his mixed-up feelings, he dreaded anything happening to this amazing woman.

'Of course. I'm sorry. Please come in,' Eve said. 'It's been a hectic day and I've had a lot on my mind.'

'What would you like me do first?' David asked.

'Would you open the boxes of glasses and give them a rinse, please? I've been so busy cooking today that I haven't had a chance. Most of my kitchen stuff is coming with the movers, so I've had to go out and buy some new things.'

'Oh, you should have asked me. I could have lent you some glasses and plates.'

'Thank you, but I'm sure these will all come in useful at some point. I'll probably have more parties and I wouldn't want to use my best crockery.'

As they worked together, Eve thought how pleasant it was and how she was looking forward to the evening. She had already decided she would be careful when talking about the murder, not wanting David to be cross with her again, especially as things were getting better between them now.

She conceded privately that she would be happier if she forgot about searching for John's killer, but she was desperate to solve the crime and prove to everyone how smart she was.

Eve glanced at David and felt warm inside. It had been a good idea to move to Crete, after all. She had started to think that life here might be dull, but it was proving to be nothing of the sort.

'Where do you want these?' David's velvety voice broke into her thoughts.

'Oh, on that table there, thanks. I must go and check on my quiches. They should be ready by now.'

Eve had surprised David again. He didn't think she would actually be cooking this evening. She really was the most intriguing woman he'd ever met. He hoped that perhaps she would cook him a meal one evening.

*   *   *

It was only just after six when the first guests arrived. Eve never failed to be surprised when people arrived dead on time at a party. She herself liked to be fashionably late whenever she went anywhere.

She greeted Pete and Annie, thinking they looked very smart this evening and was glad that they had made the effort, believing it was her influence on them that had inspired the change in their appearance. Pete handed Eve a bottle of local wine, while Annie went to put some mini quiches on the table.

'Thank you, but you needn't have bothered, Annie. I've made my own,' Eve said, slightly sharply. She knew she should be more gracious, but this was her party and she wanted the guests to praise *her* cooking. What if Annie's quiches were better than hers?

Annie wondered whether Eve had really made her own quiches, remembering that she had told her once that cooking wasn't her strongest point.

'You can never have too much food at a party round here,' she answered cheerily, attempting to defuse the situation. 'Most of the people we know will do almost anything for a free meal. I'm sure that your quiches are delicious. I just wanted to bring something to thank you for inviting us.'

Eve knew she had overreacted. Of course Annie didn't have an ulterior motive. Now, if it had been Betty, it would be a different matter. Eve went over and gave Annie a hug, surprising her with such a show of affection.

The other guests soon started to arrive, and as usual, Phyllis accompanied Don and Betty. Ken and Jan had shut the bar for a couple of hours to come to the party, knowing that most of their regulars would be at Eve's anyway. David served the drinks and Eve went round with the food, making sure everybody knew she had cooked it herself.

The drink flowed and soon the guests began to unwind. When Eve put on some music, Ken and Jan started to dance and were soon joined by Pete and Annie. Eve was in her element socialising and David admired the way she had so easily turned into the perfect hostess. He wished he could be as comfortable as she was in company. Surprisingly, the only time he was ever able to feel relaxed with others was when he was on stage.

David was also relieved that Eve hadn't mentioned John so far — and neither had anyone else — but he had a feeling that this peace wouldn't last long.

There was another knock at the door and David went to answer it. Yiannis and Laura came in, followed by Petros and a couple of the Greek men who had worked for John. Eve glared at them. She had invited Laura and knew she would bring Yiannis, but she hadn't asked the others. Still, it could prove useful in finding out more about John, so she put on a smile and went to shake hands with them, but before she could say anything, Betty's overpowering voice filled the room.

'Petros! How nice to see you! I was so pleased to hear that the police had released you. We all knew you hadn't killed John. You really had nothing to gain, did you? After all, none of you have worked since his death, have you?'

'No, we haven't. And not only that, but John hadn't paid us for weeks, so things are a bit hard for all of us.'

Petros spoke excellent English and Eve wondered if he had learnt it at school, thinking it was much easier to learn languages as a child. What chance did any of them have of learning Greek at their age? Not to mention the fact that it was even a different alphabet!

'I'm sure you'll all get your back wages from John's estate or from whoever takes over,' Annie interjected.

As usual, Annie was being optimistic, but unfortunately nobody else shared her hopes.

'There's little chance of that,' Petros replied. 'John had financial problems and owed the banks a lot of money. I doubt if there'll be anything left for wages — or for finishing your homes, come to that.'

'I don't believe it,' Betty said, her voice trembling.

She was almost in tears, surprising even Eve.

'No — I take it back,' Betty continued. 'I *do* believe it. I knew he was no good! We'll have to go and see a lawyer, won't we, Don? Perhaps if all of us affected by this go together, we can put on some pressure.'

'It probably won't do any good,' Don said philosophically, putting his arms around his wife.

Don was a quiet man and Eve had very rarely heard him speak. She looked at Don and Betty and wondered if perhaps they had financial problems themselves. It dawned on her how lucky she was.

'We put all our savings into that house and we're living here on our pensions,' Betty said, tears beginning to fall. 'We haven't got the money to finish our home now. Everything's got so expensive here since the economic crisis started and we're struggling to make ends meet. What are we going to do, Don?'

Betty was a proud woman and Eve was startled that she had admitted they had money worries. Seeing how serious everybody in the room had become, Eve wondered whether many of them had the same problems. She didn't often think about poverty, but that wasn't because she didn't care. She and her friends didn't have these concerns, and even her previous clients were generally successful actors.

For a moment, she felt ashamed that she had thought Betty, or indeed any of the ex-pats, had killed John. They were just ordinary people who had wanted to start a new and better life. Perhaps she should give up her search for the killer and leave it to the police after all?

'Well, I'm not sorry he's dead. He got everything he deserved,' Yiannis broke in. 'Pursuing women half his age. Not finishing houses. Not paying his bills. He should have been chased out of this country years ago.'

As he spoke, Eve's interest in finding the killer rushed back.

'You should be careful what you say, Yiannis,' she remarked. 'People will think you have something to hide.'

Yiannis turned his piercing eyes on her.

'I've heard you've been going round accusing people of John's murder. You should be more careful — you could upset the wrong people.'

'I haven't accused anyone of murdering John. People gossip too much. I wasn't even on Crete when he died, so how would I know?' Eve retorted.

'Women like you can't help but interfere. You think you know everything,' Yiannis hissed. He grabbed Eve's arm and stared intently into her eyes.

David and Pete immediately ran towards them and pulled Yiannis away from Eve.

'Hey, that's enough, Yiannis,' Pete said sternly. 'I don't think Eve was accusing you of anything, but I wouldn't let the police hear you talk like this. And anyway, you're a guest in Eve's home and I'd thank you to be more polite.'

'Once a policeman, always a policeman,' Yiannis retorted. 'And, anyway, the police have questioned me already. I was out with my brother, Stelios, the night John was murdered. I have a solid alibi. Perhaps it was Laura who killed

John. She was at work until nine and could have popped in and finished him off on the way back home.' He laughed. 'As if a waif like her could kill a man the size of John! But Eve will probably think it's her now. Let's go somewhere else, Laura. I'm bored of this party.'

Laura looked ready to cry, but she moved quickly towards Eve. 'I'm sorry about Yiannis,' she said quietly. 'He's had a bit too much to drink. He's not always . . . '

'Laura, I said we're going,' Yiannis butted in.

He took her arm and didn't allow her to say anything else. Within a few moments, they had left.

Eve sat down, shaking. Although she had hoped she might learn something about the night of John's murder, she hadn't expected anything spectacular to happen, and she certainly hadn't anticipated an outburst from Yiannis.

He definitely hadn't forgotten that John had made a play for Laura. Eve decided that she didn't like him at all.

He had an awful temper, and on top of it all he was a bully. Her fears about Yiannis's mistreatment of Laura had been proven right.

David glanced at Eve; she was looking pale, despite her tan. Noticing that she was trembling, he brought her a Metaxa, hoping that the Greek brandy would calm her down.

'Here, drink this. You'll feel better.'

'Thanks, David.' She sighed. 'I must try to be more careful in what I say. I really wasn't accusing him, though. I was just saying . . . '

'Yes, you do seem to keep putting your foot in it, don't you?' chipped in Betty. 'Mind you, I wouldn't trust him either. I've heard that he used to slap his previous girlfriend around. I think Laura needs to give him the push.'

Eve took a sip of Metaxa. It was sweeter than normal brandy, but she found it very soothing. It had given her a shock when Yiannis had grabbed her arm, but she'd stopped shaking now and had started thinking about the murder again.

If Yiannis hadn't had an alibi for the night of John's murder, she would have put him at the top of her suspect list — but was the alibi to be trusted? Yiannis could have persuaded his brother to lie for him, after all — Greek families stuck together.

David realised that Eve's mind was ticking over again. He'd almost hoped she had been frightened enough to stop thinking about John's murder, but to his dismay he could see that she had recovered from the shock already.

'I hope you're not thinking that Yiannis killed John,' David said quietly to Eve. 'He does have an alibi, you know.'

'What if his brother is lying?'

'I'm sure the police will find out if he is. Yiannis isn't a nice man and you need to be careful around him. He flares up so quickly and things could easily get more than a little unpleasant. He's always getting into fights and upsetting people.'

Eve was certain now that David did care for her. She was delighted that he was worried that something could happen to her. She wished that everybody would go home apart from him, but Pete was pouring out more drinks.

'What about Laura, then? She could have killed him on the way back from work, just as Yiannis said,' Eve continued.

'She can't weigh more than seven stone, so it's not likely she'd have the strength.'

'You're probably right.' Eve sighed. 'And I doubt she'd kill him just because he'd made a pass at her. Though perhaps Yiannis gave her so much grief over it that she wanted John out of the way.'

'Are you okay?' Annie asked, coming over to Eve. 'I was worried when Yiannis grabbed you. I've seen his temper before. It just seems to come out of nowhere.'

Eve thought how kind and concerned everybody was being. She hadn't had many close friends before and this was a new experience. She started thinking that perhaps she should listen to David and put all thoughts of the murder behind her.

Maybe she should just concentrate on a new and peaceful life . . . but then the room suddenly started to spin and Eve collapsed to the floor.

7

Eve woke up in bed feeling nauseous and weak. She couldn't remember how she had got there and was surprised to see Phyllis sitting by her side, reading a magazine.

'How are you?' Phyllis asked; realising that Eve was awake. 'We were all worried about you.'

Eve stared at her, trying to make out what had happened.

'I think I'm okay, but I do feel a bit dizzy and sick,' she replied after a moment. 'I remember the party and feeling ill, but not much after that. How did I get here?'

'David carried you up. He was very concerned.'

Eve suddenly felt better and tried to sit up. 'Where is he? I'd like to thank him.'

'Oh, he left a little while ago. Annie

and I said we'd keep an eye on you. She's clearing up downstairs.'

Eve wondered why David hadn't stayed, but then she felt sick again and thought it was probably best that he didn't see her like this — her hair was probably a mess as well. 'What time is it?' she asked Phyllis.

'Just after midnight.'

Eve hadn't realised she'd been asleep for so long, so imagined that David had probably thought she wouldn't wake until morning. It had been around eight when Yiannis and Laura had left.

Eve started to think about the party. She hadn't had that much to drink, so what could have made her pass out?

'Thanks for staying, Phyllis. Sorry about the evening being ruined. I thought the party was going so well, but then Yiannis lost his temper and everything went wrong after that.'

'It's not your fault,' Phyllis replied. 'Yiannis is a very volatile man. Poor Laura. She has to put up with a lot from him.'

'Good thing she has you as a friend.'

'Me? What do you mean? I'm afraid I don't know her at all, except by sight.'

'Oh, I'm sorry,' Eve replied. 'Pete and Annie were giving me a lift home from Hari's a few days ago and I thought I saw her going into your house.'

Phyllis thought for a moment before speaking.

'I don't have many visitors, so let me think back.' She paused again before she went on. 'Oh, I remember — a young tourist did knock at my door a couple of days ago to ask for a drink. She was out hiking and had run out of water. If I remember rightly, she was very small and thin like Laura.'

'That must have been her, then,' Eve replied. 'I couldn't see clearly. We were going a bit too fast and I had indulged in a few rakis! But talking about Laura, I think I'll try and see if I can have a bit of a chat with her. I do think she needs a friend. That is, if I can get past Yiannis.'

Eve lay back on her pillow; she still felt sick and miserable. She had been looking forward to spending some time alone with David at the end of the evening, but that chance had disappeared. Mind you, it seemed quite likely that he would come and visit tomorrow to see how she was, so things weren't completely bleak. Thinking about him, she closed her eyes and drifted off to sleep again.

*   *   *

Eve didn't wake until the following morning.

Feeling better, she decided to go downstairs for a cup of tea, but as she walked by the lounge, she saw a figure lying on the sofa. She stopped, her heart beginning to pound, but then she saw it was Annie.

Eve went over and shook her gently, hoping not to startle her.

'Haven't you been home yet?' she asked quietly. Annie still had on the same clothes that she had worn the night before.

'I was worried about you,' Annie replied, yawning. 'I didn't plan to spend the night here; I must have dozed off.'

Eve felt lucky that she had made new friends so quickly. She wouldn't admit it to anyone, but she knew that most of the people she mixed with in England were rather superficial.

All of a sudden, Eve's head started to spin again and her stomach hurt; she rushed to the bathroom, and after being violently sick, felt so weak that she struggled to get back into the lounge before she collapsed in a heap in a chair.

'I didn't have a lot to drink last night,' she told Annie. 'I don't know what it is, but I feel awful.'

Annie went to the kitchen and poured Eve a glass of water.

'I really don't feel well, Annie,' Eve muttered. 'I still feel sick and my head hurts. What on earth is wrong with me?' She hated feeling ill and not being in control.

'Come on, I'm taking you to the hospital,' Annie declared.

'No way!' Eve replied sharply. 'I'm sure it's not necessary, and anyway I'm not going to a Greek hospital.'

'You really aren't well at all, Eve,' Annie pointed out. 'And as it's Sunday there won't be any surgeries open, so it will have to be the hospital. Pete and I have both been there and it's fine. The doctors all speak English, so you have nothing to worry about. I'll just nip home and get my car.'

'Okay,' Eve said reluctantly, 'but I'll have to go and put on some make-up. I'm not going out looking like this.'

Annie grinned. Eve could be at death's door, yet she would still be worried about her appearance.

* * *

Twenty minutes later, Eve came down the stairs, looking brighter, but Annie suspected that it was just the make-up.

'How are you feeling now?' she asked.

'Worse,' Eve replied. 'I've just been sick again.'

'Come on, let's go. It won't take us long to get to the hospital. We should be there in about half an hour.'

Eve got into Annie's car. The journey seemed much longer to her than it actually was, the movement of the car making her feel even more nauseous. Luckily however, she wasn't sick in the car. Finally they arrived at Chania hospital and Eve was grateful that Annie was with her and knew where she was going.

While they were waiting to see the doctor, Eve noticed Laura walking into the emergency room and she nudged Annie.

'Look — it's Laura. Good grief! She's got a black eye and bruises all over one arm. I bet that's Yiannis's doing. I'm going over to talk to her.'

'Don't,' Annie replied quickly. 'For all you know, Yiannis has come with her. He's already angry with you and you don't know what he might do. You need to be careful.'

'He won't have come if he's done that to her and anyway, what about Laura? Somebody has to help her.'

'Well, wait a minute and see if Yiannis turns up. Besides, for all you know, she could just have fallen over.'

Eve knew that was unlikely and she refused to wait for more than a few minutes, but she returned from speaking to Laura quite quickly.

'She says she fell down the stairs, but I know she's lying. What are we going to do, Annie?'

'I have no idea. If Laura won't press charges, then there's nothing we can do.'

Their conversation was interrupted by the arrival of a doctor and Eve was relieved that he did speak English. She was given blood tests and asked for a sample, and when she was sick again, the doctor decided that it would be best to keep her in. Eve started to protest, but Annie was determined to take charge. They'd have the results of her tests by the end of the day, and she needed to remain in hospital in case there was something seriously wrong with her.

'Come on,' Annie urged. 'It's the sensible thing to do. You don't want to go home and then have to come back. Give me your keys and I'll come back with some night clothes.'

'And please feed Portia, she'll be hungry,' Eve pleaded.

Eve was taken to a small ward where there were just four beds, two of which were occupied by elderly Greek women. All of a sudden, Eve felt homesick. She had only left England a few days previously to live in a foreign country, and now she was in a Greek hospital, with two old women who probably couldn't speak English.

Feeling a tear fall down her cheek, she quickly wiped it away. It wasn't often that Eve cried, but she now felt out of her depth.

As if she could sense her distress, one of the Greek women got out of bed and slowly walked towards her. She put her wrinkled hand over Eve's and smiled kindly.

Eve looked at her and felt guilty. She often criticised the Greeks, yet this woman was treating her like a friend. Eve tried to thank her in broken Greek, and the woman smiled again before returning to her bed.

Eve lay down, her head spinning again. She felt very tired.

★　★　★

When Eve woke up, Annie was sitting by the side of her bed with Pete standing behind her.

'You're looking a little better,' Annie remarked, smiling.

'I've had a good sleep and yes, I don't feel sick any more. Perhaps you should take me home now.'

'Not so fast,' Pete said. 'They'll have the results of your tests later in the day, so you need to stay until then.'

Surprisingly, Eve agreed. She knew they were right, and despite her improvement, she was still a little tired and didn't have the energy to argue.

'How's Portia? I hope she doesn't think I've abandoned her.'

'Portia's fine. I've fed and walked her and left her asleep in her basket,' Annie reassured her.

Eve wanted to ask whether they had told David, but she didn't want them to think she was chasing him.

'Here's the stuff you asked for,' Annie added. 'We have to pop into Chania now, but we'll be back later to see if the results have come through. You'll be okay, won't you?'

'Of course, I'll be fine,' Eve replied, stifling a yawn. She was still feeling tired and thought it would be a good idea if she put on her nightdress and got into bed properly.

'Oh, by the way,' Annie said as they were leaving. 'I told David what had happened. He said to tell you he'll be along to see you later this afternoon.'

Despite the inconvenience of being ill, Eve thought that the hospital stay could have some advantages after all. David would be even more sympathetic, and they might become closer.

She hoped she'd manage to stay awake for his arrival, but her eyelids were drooping. She went into the bathroom to get changed and then collapsed into bed.

★ ★ ★

When Eve woke a couple of hours later, she felt refreshed. She saw Annie and Pete sitting by the side of her bed again — and then she noticed David. She thought it just might have been worth getting sick just to have him at her hospital bedside. She tried to sit up, but found it was harder than she expected.

'How are you feeling?' David asked, taking her hand. 'We were all very concerned.'

'You've got a bit more colour in you

than you had this morning,' Annie continued. 'You have such a good tan that it was strange to see you looking so drained.'

'I'm feeling better, thank you,' Eve answered, trembling at David's touch. 'I think I'll get up and go home.'

'You'll do no such thing,' David said sternly. 'The doctors need to check you over before you leave, and anyway, they haven't given you the results of the tests yet.'

Eve was delighted that David was giving her so much attention. She was used to taking care of herself and was proud of her independence and self-sufficiency, but she certainly didn't mind David coming over all forcefully protective.

Although she preferred to be in charge of her own life and didn't enjoy being told what to do, this was different. She was ill and David was looking after her. It was perfectly natural — and if he weren't well, she would take care of him in the same way.

Pete decided to try and find out what was going on with Eve's tests, but he soon returned to the ward.

'Can't find anybody to get information from,' he remarked. 'I would think that the results would be ready by now.'

'I'm starting to feel hungry,' Eve broke in. 'I haven't eaten anything all day.'

'Oh, I forgot, I got you these,' David said, handing her a box of chocolates. 'They should keep you going until they bring some food. Mind you, don't eat too many at once. They might make you sick again. I should really have brought you some fruit. I wasn't thinking straight.'

Eve found herself blushing and thought that David was being the perfect gentleman. She was about to take his hand to thank him, when the doctor walked in and they all looked at him as he spoke very seriously.

'I'm afraid I have some bad news,' he said. 'We found traces of arsenic in your sample, Miss Masters. I take it you haven't been administering it to your-self?'

'No, of course not! Why on earth would I want to do that?' Eve exclaimed, looking even paler than before. 'Oh — someone tried to kill me! It must have happened at the party. John's killer was there and he wanted me out of the way because I was asking questions. Oh no — I feel sick again. I promise you all that I'll never interfere again.'

'As whoever poisoned you didn't administer a fatal dose, they may have been attempting to just make you ill,' the doctor continued. 'A lot of people wouldn't come to hospital if they were just being sick, so we were lucky. A build-up of arsenic is more difficult to detect and it's much easier to discover if you are tested straight away. Of course, they could have underestimated the amount of arsenic they gave you and had been attempting to kill you.'

'Oh, Annie, I didn't want to come to the hospital, did I?' Eve said, almost in tears. 'Thank you so much for persuading me. Who could it have done it?'

'I think you really should leave this to the police now,' David said grimly. 'You have to be careful, Eve. No more poking your nose into things that don't concern you.'

'Yes,' the doctor agreed. 'You must be very cautious, and I must call the police, I'm afraid — they have to be informed. Didn't I read in the newspaper that an Englishman was recently murdered in your village?'

'Yes,' Eve said, 'but the police think it was simply a robbery gone wrong.'

'I think they may change their minds now,' the doctor continued. 'I will go and call them and you, Miss Masters, will have to stay here overnight. We need to keep an eye on you.'

Eve was about to protest, but the doctor was already leaving the ward.

'I want to go home,' she said, almost in tears.

'Don't worry,' David said sympathetically. 'I'm sure it'll only be for one night. They just want to make certain. We'll stay with you for a while, won't we, Annie?'

'We don't have to go until the police have been,' Annie agreed. 'I want to hear what they have to say, anyway. One good thing about this hospital is that visitors can stay as long as they want to.'

Eve looked at the Greek women on the other side of the ward. The husband of one of them looked as if he had settled down for the night, and six members of the other woman's family surrounded her. Seeing how much family meant to the Greeks, Eve felt herself softening towards them. Greek children looked after their parents and didn't put them into a nursing home when they grew old.

Suddenly, she wished more than anything that she had a loving family. She wasn't at all close to her own parents; they had sent her away to boarding schools from the age of seven.

As she settled back down in bed, she

thought how comfortable it was in this hospital. There was a warm and relaxed atmosphere in the ward, and best of all, David was sitting at her bedside and had said he would stay as long as she needed him.

She wasn't looking forward to seeing the police and wondered if they would be able to speak English. Eve suddenly felt tired again, and although she tried to keep her eyes open, she drifted back off to sleep.

★　★　★

It was starting to get dark when Eve woke up again. Looking around, she saw two policemen in the ward. When she heard them talking in English to her friends, she was relieved, having heard that many police officers only spoke Greek.

She'd hoped that some of the police force must have knowledge of other languages. After all, this was a holiday island and foreigners could easily be involved in crimes, not to mention car accidents. Although she hadn't been driving on Crete for long, she had noticed that the standard of driving wasn't that high, and she usually felt lucky to reach her destination without being involved in an accident.

One of the policemen noticed that Eve was awake and went over to her. 'Good evening, madam. You have had a fortunate escape, I think.'

'I know. Someone poisoned me.'

'Yes, your companions have been filling me in. I hear that you were trying to find out who murdered John Phillips. You know, you should leave the investigating to the police. That's what we're here for.'

Eve was irritated and wanted to say that she didn't think they were interested in finding out who had murdered John, but for once she held back, thinking it advisable not to alienate the police in a foreign country.

'I only asked a few questions, nothing more,' she lied. 'I'm so sorry. I won't do it again. I was just being curious.'

Annie and David glanced at each other, both certain that Eve wouldn't give up, especially as her life had been threatened. However, they were anxious. Somebody had attempted to hurt, or even kill Eve, and he or she might try again. Annie wondered whether it had just been a warning — or if the person had really wanted to kill Eve and had failed.

'Would you look at this list, Miss Masters?' the police officer continued. 'Your friends say these were the people at your party. Have they forgotten anyone? We intend to question each person in turn as soon as possible.'

Eve studied the piece of paper. 'No, that's everybody.'

'Mr Baker says that you had an argument with Yiannis Neonaki. I believe he physically attacked you before he left with his girlfriend, Miss Laura James?'

'Yes, we had words and he grabbed my arm. I didn't accuse him of murdering John. I only said that he should watch what he said. He more or less indicated that John deserved to die because he made a pass at Laura and hadn't finished building houses on time. I must admit that Yiannis did scare me and I was glad I wasn't on my own with him. He has an awful temper and he did hurt me when he grabbed me.'

'You need to be more careful. In the light of what happened to you, it seems it could have been someone at your party who killed John and now they're after you. However, I think it will be difficult to discover who did this. It wouldn't have been too hard for someone to put arsenic in your drink, but you never know, perhaps somebody noticed something unusual.'

'One other thing,' Eve said quickly, interrupting the police officer before he could say anything else. 'It's about Yiannis.'

Out of the corner of her eye, Eve could see Annie shaking her head, but she pretended not to notice and carried on.

'When Annie and I were in emergency downstairs, we saw Laura, his girlfriend, and she had a black eye and bruises all over her arm. Yiannis treats her terribly and I'm sure he did this, but she says she just fell down the stairs.'

'I'm sorry,' the policeman replied. 'If she won't admit it's him, there's nothing we can do. If you are that certain, you must convince her to come to us, I'm afraid.'

Eve sighed, but at least the officer wasn't ignoring her suspicions completely.

'Now,' he continued. 'I will leave you in peace. You will be safe here, but I am a little worried about you living on your own.' He turned towards the others. 'Perhaps one of you could move in with Miss Masters for a few days when she gets out of hospital? It would be safer until we close this case.'

Eve suddenly became excited, thinking that David could stay with her! It would be a wonderful opportunity for them to get to know each other better. But before she was able to suggest it, Pete spoke up.

'Annie could stay with you — couldn't you, darling?'

'Yes, of course,' Annie replied, smiling.

Annie knew Eve would be disappointed, but she thought it would be for the best. She had talked to David about Eve, and he had admitted that he was very attracted to her, but also that her complexity frightened him. Sometimes he found her domineering and brusque, but then she would surprise him with her softness. She was one of the most intriguing women he had ever met, but also one of the most frustrating.

Annie believed it was too early in their relationship for them to spend too much time together and that it would be better if they did take it slowly.

'Thank you, Annie, that would be

lovely,' Eve said, trying not to look disappointed. This wasn't what she wanted, but she didn't make a fuss.

David knew Eve would have preferred him to stay with her rather than Annie, but he wasn't ready to spend so much time with her, and was relieved when Pete had suggested that Annie should move in. He admired Eve for hiding her disappointment and thought things could work out for them if they went at his pace and got to know each other properly.

'I promise I'll pop over to see you every day,' he said. 'And I'll walk Portia for you if you're not up to it.'

'Thank you, that would be lovely,' Eve replied, brightening and thinking that things weren't as hopeless as they could be.

'Anyway, it's getting late,' David remarked, seeing that Eve's eyes were getting heavy. 'Perhaps we'd better go and let you have some more rest.'

Eve didn't want him to leave, but she was feeling tired. It would probably take her a few days to get over the effects of the arsenic and flush it from her system.

'Thank you all for being here for me. I really do appreciate it,' she murmured.

Annie and Pete smiled and said their goodbyes, then David bent over and kissed her briefly, leaving the ward before she could say anything.

Eve leaned back on her pillow, feeling content. This was almost a perfect situation. She had found good friends and David had kissed her again — admittedly fleetingly, but it was the second time he had done so. He was just building up to the real kiss and she couldn't wait for it to happen! Thinking about it, she closed her eyes, but within a few minutes she sat up again, remembering that someone had poisoned her last night and she was lucky to be alive.

Eve shuddered, wishing she were back in England.

8

Back at home the following afternoon, Eve tried to relax on her sofa, but it felt lumpy and she wished her own settee would hurry up and arrive from England. She had decided that Greek sofas definitely weren't as comfortable as English ones, but then told herself to stop these comparisons. There were always going to be differences between the two countries, and while some things were superior in England to their equivalents in Greece, other things were actually better here than back home.

She had made her choice to live on Crete, having been mesmerised by the ancient Minoan palaces, the long sandy beaches and the snow-capped mountains. She had to accept that it wasn't going to be like London. Otherwise she might as well pack her bags and go back to England now.

'Don't you think you should go upstairs and lie down, Eve?' Annie asked, thinking that she still looked pale.

'I've spent enough time in bed over the last couple of days,' Eve replied. 'I'll be fine here.'

At that moment, they both heard barking and Annie hurried to let Portia into the room.

'Are you sure that you want to have an indoor dog?' Annie asked. 'Lots of people in Greece keep their dogs in kennels outside. It's not as if the weather's the same as in England. She's probably not house-trained and it's much harder to teach an older dog than a young pup. And you do have a big garden for her to run about in.'

'This poor dog needs a loving home and I'm not leaving her outside all day,' Eve replied firmly.

Annie smiled, thinking that there really was some tenderness underneath that brusque exterior. She wondered about Eve's past, trying to imagine what had happened to make her act the way she did. Annie didn't think Eve was a bad person at all, and hoped she would soon open up to her.

'Look, I have to pop home and get a few clothes to tide me over,' Annie told Eve. 'Will you be okay here on your own just for a little while? I'll only be gone for about half an hour at the most.'

'I'll be fine, Annie, honestly. I have Portia to protect me.'

After Annie had left, Eve stroked her dog affectionately, but started to shiver despite the heat. Although she didn't want to admit it, she was nervous. Someone had attempted to make her very sick, or more likely even kill her, and they could attempt to hurt her again. She jumped as she heard a knock at the door, but then she heard Betty's voice.

'I've just seen Annie. She told me you were home.'

Eve got up slowly and went to the door.

'Come in, both of you,' Eve said reluctantly, noticing that Phyllis was there as well. 'Sorry I took so long. I'm still feeling weak, not to mention a bit uneasy about all this. I'm glad that Annie's staying with me for a few days.'

'Yes, it's very kind of her,' Betty replied. 'It must have been a shock to find out that someone wanted you dead.'

Betty often spoke without thinking, and Eve thought a remark like this was quite uncalled-for. It reminded her starkly of what had happened and she really wanted to put it all behind her and get on with life. Why on earth had Betty bothered to visit? After all, she didn't like her, and it was probably just for show — or, more likely, to be nosey.

Eve wished that Phyllis wouldn't hide behind Betty all the time. She wanted to shake her and tell her to get a grip. After all, her husband had been dead for eight months and surely it was time she started to move on.

But perhaps she had adored him and

life was too difficult on her own, Eve reminded herself. Who knew? Phyllis never gave anything away, and Eve wondered whether even Betty knew much about her.

'Phyllis, go and put the kettle on, there's a dear.' Betty's annoying voice interrupted Eve's thoughts. 'I think we could all manage a cup of tea.'

'Oh no, it's all right. I'll do it,' Eve interjected.

'Don't be silly,' Betty continued. 'You need to rest. I'm sure you'll be fine in a couple of days, but you mustn't overdo things.'

Eve sat back down. Being waited on would be nice for a while, but she liked her independence and didn't want this to go on for too long. It was also irritating to hear Betty bossing Phyllis around. Why couldn't Betty have made the tea herself?

'Are you sure you want to have that dog indoors?' Betty asked Eve abruptly. 'You don't know where she's come from.'

Eve was getting fed up of being told what to do with her dog. Portia was her friend and if she wanted to keep her inside, she would. However, there was no point arguing with Betty, who always thought she was right and refused to listen to anyone else's opinions.

Eve was also slightly worried about upsetting her too much — just in case she had been the one who had poisoned her and killed John! Although she hadn't put Betty at the top of her suspect list, there was still a faint possibility that she might be the culprit, and Eve thought it best to tread carefully.

'I'm taking Portia to the vet as soon as I'm better,' Eve explained. 'I'll get her checked over and make sure she has all the necessary injections.'

'She'll probably need to be spayed as well,' Betty commented. 'The Greeks generally don't bother. That's why there are so many unwanted cats and dogs wandering the streets here. It'll cost a fair bit to have all that done.'

'That won't be a problem,' Eve replied, but immediately wished she hadn't made such a thoughtless remark. Eve knew Betty and Don had financial problems, and despite not liking Betty, she didn't like flaunting her wealth.

'What I meant to say is,' Eve continued quickly, 'I've fallen in love with the dog and it'll be worth whatever it costs to have such an adorable companion.'

Betty wondered whether she had misjudged Eve. Although Eve knew that she and Don were struggling to make ends meet, she wasn't looking down on them and actually seemed almost sympathetic to their problems.

Nevertheless, Betty didn't consider the newcomer a suitable partner for David, believing she was too conceited and vain. In reality, Betty was jealous of Eve's beauty and confidence and hated David's admiration of her.

'I found these biscuits,' Phyllis ventured, returning with the tea. 'I hope it was okay to open them.'

'Yes, of course. I must admit that I am a bit hungry,' Eve replied. 'The hospital food wasn't much to write home about, but at least David brought me some delicious chocolates.'

Betty grimaced, but then remembered that her niece, Alison Taylor, was coming on holiday from England in a couple of days' time. She was younger than Eve, and although both women were attractive, Alison was a much less aggressive person.

Betty hoped that David was just being nice to Eve because of the attempt on her life. If she had seen David kiss Eve twice, she might have been more concerned. It didn't matter that both embraces were gentle and not blazing with passion; they were still kisses.

'Well, the police came to see both of us this morning,' Betty continued. 'I don't think they're any further forward. They're interviewing everybody who came to your party, but it's going to be difficult to prove anything.'

'I know,' Eve agreed despondently. 'I'm just going to have to be more careful from now on.'

'Probably best. Oh, they did ask about Yiannis and your argument, but I don't know if they suspect him. He has a reputation for getting into fights, but as far as I know, he's never seriously injured anyone.'

'They probably don't suspect him because he's Greek.'

'Possibly,' Betty answered, pursing her lips.

Eve was surprised that Betty agreed with her, but then felt guilty. Meeting the Greek women and their families in hospital had changed her attitude towards the Greek people. David had been right, and she was beginning to think that they were kind and caring people; she just had to get to know them better.

As Eve took a sip of tea, she shuddered. Although it tasted warm and comforting, she remembered that someone had slipped arsenic into her drink at the party. She looked at Betty and Phyllis sitting there innocently, but even if it had been one of them, they probably wouldn't try again today. It would be much too obvious.

The room went quiet as everyone drank their tea, but then a . . . knock at the door interrupted the silence.

'Go and get that, dear,' Betty said to Phyllis.

Eve had to stop herself from saying anything, even though she was getting more and more irritated with Betty's attitude towards Phyllis. She wondered whether Phyllis minded, or if she was just biding her time before rebelling.

Then she looked round and her green eyes widened. All thoughts of Betty and Phyllis simply disappeared.

'Hello, how are you today?' David asked. 'You look much better, though you still haven't got all your colour back.'

'I'm still a bit tired, but my appetite's returned and I haven't been sick today,' Eve replied almost coyly.

'Good. I hope these ladies aren't tiring you out too much.'

'Of course not,' Betty piped up. 'We've made the tea and Eve hasn't had to do anything. We just wanted to see if she was okay. She shouldn't really be left alone, but Annie's just popped home to get some things.'

Eve seethed inside. It was just like Betty to take some of the credit for making the tea.

'Have the police been to see you yet, Betty?' David asked.

'Yes, they have. I don't think they've got anywhere with either the murder or Eve's poisoning, but I could be wrong . . .'

'Unless somebody actually saw the person tampering with Eve's drink, it will be very difficult to prove who poisoned her,' David continued. 'After all, it could have been anybody. I don't think the police have much of a chance of finding out who did it.'

While they were talking, Annie returned. She was flustered and started talking quickly. 'I just bumped into Ken and he said the police were searching Yiannis's house. He reckons they're looking for the arsenic!'

Eve wasn't expecting this news. She was certain that the same person who had killed John had poisoned her, and the only way that it could possibly be Yiannis was if his alibi for the night of John's murder was false. Perhaps the police suspected that it was — or maybe they thought that Laura was the culprit. But would she really have been able to kill John?

'Well, this is all very interesting,' Betty remarked. 'Things are certainly heating up now. Yiannis does things on the spur of the moment, which is why he's the ideal suspect for John's murder. He could have gone over to confront John about making a move on Laura and then ended up hitting him on the head.'

'Yes,' Eve agreed reluctantly, 'but he does have an alibi for the whole evening.'

'It's gone through all of our minds that his brother could be covering up for him,' Betty replied. 'Mind you, as to poisoning you, I don't know if that's quite his thing. It seems too organised for him. He would more likely attack you down a quiet road.'

Eve was getting fed up with Betty. She was putting more and more unpleasant thoughts into her head.

'Has anyone thought that it might have been Laura who poisoned you, Eve?' Phyllis broke in. 'Perhaps she might have suspected or even known that Yiannis killed John, and when you started asking questions, she became concerned and decided to get rid of you. Despite the way he treats her, she loves him.'

Everybody turned to look at Phyllis, astonished to hear her say more than a couple of words, let alone give an opinion. Eve saw that Betty was annoyed, and thought that maybe Phyllis was more than just a shadow after all.

'Really, Phyllis,' Betty said, trying to regain control of the situation. 'You've not had much to do with Laura, but I've known her for several years. She was my rep when we first came here on holiday. She was only nineteen then and it was her first job. She's a lovely girl and I can't see her trying to kill anyone. Even if she knew that Yiannis had killed John, she'd never kill anyone herself. She's much too good for Yiannis and deserves someone who gives her a bit more respect than he does.'

'Come on, everybody!' Annie said loudly. 'We're all doing it now. We're accusing people without any real evidence. We should have learned a lesson after what happened to Eve. Whoever murdered John and poisoned Eve means business, and if we carry on like this, any one of us could be in danger.'

'You're right, Annie,' Eve said quietly. 'Since finding out about the arsenic, I'm really feeling on edge. Initially it felt like a bit of fun playing amateur detective, but in the end, it wasn't at all and I could be dead now — and what would have happened to poor Portia then?'

Eve burst into tears. David put his arms around her.

'I'd have looked after her, don't you worry,' he said soothingly, but then blurted out awkwardly, 'What am I saying? I'm so sorry, Eve. That can't have made you feel any better!'

He sat back on the arm of her chair, still with one arm across her shoulders.

'You've got to stop thinking about what happened, Eve. Someone tried to hurt you, but they didn't succeed, and with the police involved now, the person who did this will keep a low profile. As long as you keep quiet, you shouldn't be in any danger.'

David's reassurances gave Eve a wonderful warm and comfortable feeling. She wished he'd stay with her forever — but Betty wasn't going to allow that.

'Come along, David, Phyllis, we need

to get going,' she said briskly. 'Eve needs her rest. She's been through a terrible ordeal and we mustn't tire her out.'

'You're right,' David said, getting up. 'I'll come and see you later, Eve. Try to get some more sleep. I'm sure you'll be back to normal in no time at all.'

David bent over and kissed Eve lightly on the cheek. She was disappointed, thinking that if there ever was a time for him to kiss her on the lips, this was it. Eve was still brooding over the fact that Betty had missed their last two kisses.

However, Betty did look thoroughly exasperated that David had kissed her at all, and she decided that the gesture hadn't been a total let-down.

As she shut the front door behind her, Betty thought darkly that the sooner her niece came to Crete, the better. Alison was tall and beautiful, and never had a bad word to say about anyone — plus she was ten years younger than Eve. David had met her last year and had seemed interested, but she had been in a relationship then. As that was now over, the door was open for David to make a move.

Betty decided she would have to invite him to her house for dinner when her niece arrived. She felt they would make an excellent match and she smiled triumphantly at the thought of Eve's reaction.

9

After a couple of days, Eve felt much better. However the police hadn't been able to find any trace of arsenic at Yiannis's house, and he was still walking free. Eve felt uneasy, but she wasn't surprised that Yiannis hadn't been arrested. He wasn't stupid, and if he were guilty he would surely have been intelligent enough to dispose of any poison left over.

She still believed that he was the most likely suspect in both John's murder and in her poisoning, but she doubted whether Laura had anything to do with it. Phyllis seemed to think that she might be involved, but Eve thought that Laura had become too frightened to try anything.

As Eve's health improved, she started to get bored at home, and she was also upset that David hadn't been to see her as often as she'd expected.

'He's reached the last few chapters of his novel,' Annie explained patiently. 'He needs to get it finished without losing momentum. Then I'm sure he'll have much more time to spend with you.'

Eve had shown Annie a kinder and more compassionate side of her character, but she could still be self-centred. For the most part, Annie had enjoyed staying with her, finding her both entertaining and interesting. Eve had led an exciting life and had told Annie stories about her time as a showbiz agent and her travels around the world — but she could also be unreasonably demanding.

'I am grateful, I really am,' Eve said quickly. 'I'm sorry if I sounded selfish.'

It was as if she could read Annie's thoughts. Eve knew she could be difficult, but in her business back in England, she had people running to do exactly what she had asked of them and she was finding it hard to change old habits.

'I know you appreciate everything we've done for you,' Annie replied, pleased to see that Eve was making an effort. 'And I know it's been hard for you, especially as you've only recently arrived here on Crete. It's not exactly been the best welcome.'

'I'm just going a bit stir crazy,' Eve moaned. 'I'm not used to being stuck indoors for such a long time. I've hardly had a day off sick all my life. Perhaps I should take Portia for a little walk.'

'Good idea. Would you like me to come with you?'

'Thanks, but no; I'll be all right. I've got to start doing things on my own again.'

Eve wouldn't admit it, but she was a little scared. However, once she was out in the sun with Portia, she didn't feel quite so bad. It was such a beautiful day, and anyway, who would attack her in broad daylight in the middle of the village? Perhaps she should stop trying to find the killer, and then she wouldn't have to look over her shoulder all the time.

Eve decided to walk to the other side of the village, thinking that would probably be enough for today.

An old Greek lady dressed completely in black sat outside her house in the shade and called out 'Kalimera', the Greek for good morning, to Eve as she walked by.

Eve smiled and replied, 'Kalimera.' She was quite proud of the number of Greek words she had already picked up, having completely forgotten that she had resolved not to bother attempting to learn Greek. In fact, she had even decided to enrol in a language school in Chania so she could be taught the language properly.

As she approached the local shop, Eve thought about stopping to get a cold drink, and then she noticed two women standing outside the door engaged in what looked like a very intense conversation.

As she got nearer, she realised it was Phyllis and Laura. She was surprised to see them talking so heatedly. Phyllis had said she didn't know Laura to talk to, but with everything that had been going on recently, Eve imagined all the ex-pats would be discussing the crimes, whether they knew each other well or not.

However, Phyllis and Laura stopped talking abruptly when they saw Eve and she surmised they were probably talking about her — imagining, as always, that she was the centre of attention.

'Good morning,' Eve said, trying to sound bright and casual. 'How are you both? This is my first day out since I was in hospital and it does feel good to get some fresh air.'

'You certainly do look a little brighter,' Phyllis answered rather awkwardly. 'It's nice to see you up and about so soon.'

'Yes, I feel a lot better, though I still haven't got all my energy back.' She turned to Laura and added, 'Your eye

130

seems to have gone down, Laura.'

Laura tried to smile, but found it practically impossible, and Eve knew she had hit a raw nerve. 'Yes, I'll have to be careful how I walk down stairs in future,' she murmured quietly. 'Sorry, I must go. Yiannis is waiting for me at home.'

Laura rushed off, head bowed, and Eve felt herself shiver, a sense of foreboding overwhelming her.

'I'm so worried about her,' Eve said, turning to Phyllis. 'She used to be so full of life and now she always looks sad and frightened. Did she say anything about Yiannis to you?'

'No. We were just talking about her job. They weren't too happy about her black eye, even though she did say she fell down,' Phyllis replied. 'I agree she does need to get rid of Yiannis, but she says she still loves him. Some women are just victims, I suppose. If you'll excuse me, I must go — I was supposed to be at Betty's ten minutes ago.'

Eve watched Phyllis leave. That was the pot calling the kettle black; if ever there was another victim, it was Phyllis.

After buying a refreshing cold drink, Eve walked home slowly, arriving home about twenty minutes later, where Annie greeted her with a cup of tea.

'I really enjoyed my walk, Annie. It was lovely to get out.'

'Tell you what,' Annie replied. 'Seeing as you're feeling better, how about a visit to The Black Cat tonight? I'll give David a ring and see if he can make it, too.'

Eve desperately wanted to see David, but she didn't want to seem pushy and phone him herself, so she was delighted that Annie had made the suggestion and taken the pressure off her.

* * *

The day went by slowly, but at last it was early evening and time for Eve to get ready. She wanted to look perfect just in case David was at The Black

Cat. He had told Annie that he couldn't promise, but he would try and make it. As Eve left the bathroom, she had a final glance in the mirror and thought she looked much better than she had a couple of days ago. Her colour had come back, and because she hadn't eaten much in hospital, her stomach was completely flat.

When Eve came downstairs, Pete had already arrived to pick them up for the evening.

'Sorry to keep you waiting,' Eve apologised.

'That's fine. I haven't been here long. I must say, Eve, you look more like your old self again.'

'Thanks. I feel a lot better, but I am a little nervous about going out. The person who poisoned me might be there.'

'I doubt if he or she would try anything in a public bar,' Pete replied reassuringly.

'You're probably right. It just makes me feel a bit jumpy thinking about it.'

'Just don't mention John and the murder. Don't give anyone an excuse to do anything.'

'Believe me, I won't. I promise I've abandoned my ideas about being a detective. It's much too risky.'

Eve noticed Annie was smiling and realised she hadn't fooled her. Eve had tried to avoid talking about the murder in the last couple of days, but the conversation had occasionally drifted back to it and Annie knew that Eve was still keenly interested in solving the case herself.

'Come on, let's go,' Pete urged. 'I've brought the car just in case you're tired later on, Eve.'

A few minutes later they walked into the bar. Ken was clearing tables, but he rushed over to Eve and gave her a hug, making her feel terrible that it had ever crossed her mind that he had murdered John.

'Great to see you!' he exclaimed. 'We were all so worried. No long term effects from the poison, I hope?'

'No, I don't think so. I feel like I'm almost my old self again.'

'Go and sit down. The first drinks are on the house. G and Ts for the ladies and a beer for you, Pete?'

The women went to find a table and then Eve scoured the room, looking for David. Seeing him, she was about to shout out, when she noticed that he wasn't alone. Apart from Betty and Don, there was a beautiful dark-haired woman sitting next to him.

Who was she? David was laughing and chatting to her, and immediately Eve was filled with fury. How dare he? She had almost died, and now he was flirting with someone else — and in front of her, too! She tried to calm down, determined that David wouldn't see that she was jealous.

'Who's that sitting with David?' she asked Annie, trying to keep her voice steady.

'That's Alison, Betty's niece from England. She's visiting for a week. I remember we met her last year.'

David was only talking to Alison, but Annie was concerned, knowing how unpredictable Eve could be. How would she react?

Perhaps she would accept that Alison was just a friend, but on the other hand, she might think David was interested in her and attempt to stir things up. Annie was determined to stop her from doing anything too foolhardy, but once Eve decided to do something, Annie knew it would be difficult to stop her.

However, instead of focusing on David, Eve noticed Yiannis and Laura sitting at the bar. She marched over to them.

'Oh no,' Yiannis exclaimed. 'Trouble's here again.'

'You think you can get away with anything, Yiannis. I have no idea if you killed John or poisoned me, but I'm certain you hit Laura and so is everyone else! All you are is a bully!'

Yiannis stood up meancingly. 'You need to keep your mouth shut,' he hissed and moved towards her.

However, before he could touch her, Pete jumped up and pulled Eve away. 'Come on, Eve — come and sit back down.'

Eve allowed Pete to lead her away. She knew she was being stupid and had only confronted Yiannis because she was angry with David. When they returned to their table, David had come across to ask them to join him. Although Eve was about to refuse, both Annie and Pete accepted and Eve had no choice but to follow.

'So, what was that about, Eve?' David asked when they had sat down. 'Why did you confront Yiannis? You know you have got to be careful with him. He has a terrible temper.'

'Yes, you're playing with fire,' Betty said loudly. 'Even if he hasn't killed anyone, he could still hurt you, you know.'

'Well, none of you seem to care about Laura. Look at her. She's like a frightened little mouse,' Eve said defensively.

'We know,' agreed Annie. 'But she won't press charges and she won't leave Yiannis, so our hands are tied.'

Eve took a large gulp of her gin and tonic. What an awful evening this was turning out to be! Yiannis had nearly attacked her again through her own stupid fault and David was flirting with another woman.

How could David be so fickle? A few days ago he had been concerned about her, but now he didn't care and was all over this girl. It didn't even cross her mind that she was being irrational. After all, David had only been talking to Alison.

'Sorry, Alison, I haven't introduced you,' David said. 'This is Eve. You remember Annie and Pete, don't you?'

'Eve, what a pleasure. I've been told so much about you,' Alison said, smiling. 'I hear you've had an awful time recently. I don't know how I'd cope if someone poisoned me. I think I'd probably pack up and go back to England. You really are brave.'

Eve wondered if Alison was really concerned or if she was just trying to impress David. Not that it would take much; Alison was beautiful and confident and couldn't be much over thirty.

Eve suddenly felt old, and although she didn't usually give up on what she wanted, at this moment she felt as if she had lost David forever. Perhaps it was the effect of the last few days. After all, someone had poisoned her and that hadn't done a lot for her confidence.

She took another gulp of her G and T and felt a little better.

'Yes, Alison, it was a bit of a trial, but I got through it,' she said, trying to sound confident. 'No point brooding, after all. Got to get on with life. After all, I'm lucky to be alive.'

Annie took a large sip of her drink as well. She was still on edge, not knowing how this evening would end.

David had been keen on Alison last year, and now that her previous relationship had ended, she was free. However, Annie doubted there was a future for her with David. Alison was a career woman and Annie couldn't see her moving to Crete. She adored her life in London, while David loved Greece and had said more than once that he would never live in England again. But Annie knew love could do strange things.

After all, she had never wanted to marry a policeman, knowing that the job could be dangerous, but then she had met Pete and none of that mattered. They fell in love and got married within six months and, although a couple of years later, Pete had been shot and it was touch and go whether or not he would survive, Annie never once regretted marrying him.

'Aunt Betty was telling me that you've been trying to find out who murdered John Phillips,' Alison continued, looking at Eve.

'I was, yes — but unfortunately it seems to have got me into a lot of trouble.'

'Yes, it does!' Alison replied. 'I don't blame you, though. From what I've heard, the police haven't had much success, and even if John wasn't exactly a nice guy, his murder shouldn't go unpunished.'

Eve stared at Alison. They were on the same wavelength and if she hadn't been a rival for David's affections, they could have become good friends.

Annie studied David during the conversation. He hadn't flinched when Alison had said she couldn't live on Crete. Perhaps he didn't really care about her at all? Luckily, Eve seemed miles away, but Annie was concerned. She had acted very irrationally this evening, no doubt because she had thought she was losing David, and if she did something like this again, she could put her life in danger.

David was confused. Why on earth had Eve confronted Yiannis so aggressively? She had promised to be careful around him since she had been poisoned, especially as they had both decided that Yiannis was the most likely suspect in John's murder — even though he seemingly had an alibi. She was certainly acting strangely this evening and he had no idea why she was ignoring him.

Then realisation dawned . . . He had been sitting and chatting to Alison. No, Eve can't have thought he was interested in her, surely? All he was doing was talking to her. What was wrong with Eve? Was she really that insecure, deep down?

*   *   *

After two drinks, Eve started to feel more relaxed. Greek measures were much larger than English ones and she was already quite tipsy. She had started talking about her life as a showbiz agent, making herself out to be more influential than she actually was, and Annie wished she would stop.

Betty thought David looked embarrassed and believed his interest in Eve was disappearing rapidly. However, his real motivation was to try and find an excuse to get her away on her own to reassure her about his lack of feelings for Alison.

He thought Eve was being silly, thinking he was interested in anyone else, and knew she was only talking like this because she was upset. But before he could say anything to reassure Eve, a man's voice called out at the other end of the bar.

'Eve, darling! There you are! I went to your house and you weren't there. Thought I might find you in the bar!'

Everyone in The Black Cat turned and looked at the man who had come in. Some people thought they recognised him, but they weren't sure where from. He was blond, tall, and exceptionally handsome.

Eve got up and rushed towards him. She threw her arms around him and held on tightly.

'Robert! How wonderful to see you! I've been having such an awful time and you're just the man I need to cheer me up.'

Annie turned and looked at David. He had a bemused look on his face and she shook her head, thinking that life had stopped being dull when Eve arrived on Crete. Annie had no idea where all this was going — but she was intrigued to find out.

10

Pete and Annie gave Eve and Robert a lift home. There was no need for Annie to stay with Eve any more, so she collected her things — she was curious to know more about Eve's relationship with Robert, but she couldn't just come right out and ask. She wondered whether they had been romantically involved.

Eve had seemed thrilled to see Robert and Annie wondered if there was still a spark between them. Or had Eve just put on a show for David's benefit? Eve had obviously believed that David was keen on Alison, and if she had been trying to upset him, it looked as if it had worked; Annie had seen his face fall when Eve put her arms around Robert. Eve was definitely her own worst enemy, Annie thought.

'Thank you so much for looking after me,' Eve said to Annie. 'I know it seems as if I can take care of myself, but I don't think I would have managed too well after all that's happened. I've been pretty nervous since coming out of hospital. After all, it's not every day somebody tries to kill you!'

Annie hugged Eve, thinking that she would actually miss staying with her. Eve was different, more exciting than most people she knew, but Annie was beginning to worry about her again. She had seen Eve's eyes light up when Alison had mentioned John's murder, and suspected that her days as an amateur sleuth were far from over.

'Anyway, Annie,' Eve continued, 'Robert's here now and he'll look after me. We've been friends for absolutely years, but we haven't seen each other for a while, so we've got a lot to catch up on. Besides, I'm sure Pete will be glad to have you home.'

'Yes, I think it's true that absence makes the heart grow fonder. Or perhaps it's just my cooking he's missed!'

'I'm sure he's been lonely without you,' Eve replied wistfully. 'What I wouldn't do to have a relationship like yours! You really are lucky, Annie.'

Annie, however, was slightly envious of Eve's lifestyle, even though it seemed that Eve herself wasn't satisfied with what she had. People always wanted what they didn't have, but Annie wondered whether Eve would ever be really content. She was the type of woman who always wanted something more, she guessed.

Once Annie and Pete left, Eve headed towards the drinks cabinet. 'Another G and T, Robert?'

'Love one, even though I've probably had too many already. These Greek measures are pretty generous, aren't they? But so what, I'm on holiday!'

Eve poured the drinks, feeling that she needed another one.

'I know I was a bit weepy on the phone the other day, Robert, but I didn't expect you to come over. Having said that, it's good to see you. It's been too long.'

'I was worried about you. After all, somebody did try to kill you — but you need to stop all this nonsense now. You're playing with fire if you carry on looking for the killer.'

'I know, but it's so exciting, Robert! I want to be the one to solve the murder — just think how clever David would think I am! But what does that matter now? He's got Alison . . . '

'You do talk a lot of rubbish sometimes, Eve. I certainly couldn't see anything going on between those two. They were just talking, but if you carry on acting like you have been tonight, there could be something happening between them soon.'

Eve sighed. Robert was right; she should stop searching for the killer before she got herself into more trouble, and she should definitely apologise to David for being so silly before she drove him away . . . but she didn't want to forget about solving the murder, and she had too much pride to say sorry.

Why was she so jealous? She couldn't remember ever feeling like this before — was she actually falling in love with David? She had imagined that this was going to be a mad, passionate interlude, but, perhaps for the first time in her life, she wanted more than just some diverting fun.

'I really have messed up, haven't I, Robert?' she finally said, wringing her hands. 'I've probably lost David for good after tonight.'

'Go and talk to him tomorrow. It's never too late.'

Robert was surprised to see Eve so infatuated by a man. She had always been a woman married to her career, and men had just been passing fancies to her. Robert was a reasonably successful actor and Eve had been his agent for more than fifteen years. They had become great friends and he didn't like to see her so distressed.

The following morning, Eve and Robert sat on the patio having breakfast. Eve wasn't hungry and just picked at her cereal, drinking her second black coffee of the day, while Robert ate a hearty cooked meal of sausages, bacon, eggs, mushrooms and toast.

They sat in companionable silence; neither were morning people and Eve didn't usually say anything until she'd had at least two, if not three cups of coffee. Robert had bought a newspaper at the airport the previous afternoon and he was flicking through it, while Eve thought about the evening before.

What a total disaster! She hadn't even said goodnight to David and was now regretting her decision to ignore him. She had been thoroughly immature, and if he hadn't been interested in Alison before last night, he certainly might be now.

Then she had made it worse by throwing her arms around Robert.

Whatever must David think of her?

'About time you went over to see that boyfriend of yours, isn't it?' Robert asked, grinning and interrupting her thoughts.

'Not before I've had another coffee.'

'Ah, you're just putting it off. Come on, I've never known you to shy away from anything you want.'

Eve knew Robert was right, but she was scared. She knew she'd been a prize idiot last night and didn't want to face David.

Just as Eve finally finished her coffee, there was a knock at the door. She almost hoped it would be David; it would take some of the pressure off her. But when she went to answer it, she was disappointed to see it was Betty.

The woman looked smug and Eve was even more annoyed when she just marched past her onto the patio.

'Good morning, Robert. How are you? I hope you slept well,' Betty said brightly. 'Sorry to disturb your break-fast.'

'We've just about finished,' Eve muttered, following her.

She tried not to let Betty see that she was irritated with her, but she was finding it very hard this morning to hide her feelings.

'I wanted to invite you both over to my house this evening. Don and I are having a little drinks party to welcome Alison. I hope you can come.'

Eve was about to refuse when Robert piped in with, 'We'd love to. What time?'

'Around eight. I hope Eve is taking you to see the sights this week, Robert. David has very kindly offered to drive Alison into Chania today to go round the museums. She's very interested in the history of the island. Anyway, I've lots to do, so I'll see you both later tonight.'

When Betty had left, Eve looked angrily at Robert.

'Why did you say we'd go to her party tonight? The last thing I want to do is watch David fawn over Alison all evening. I'm sure that's the only reason

Betty invited us.'

'Probably,' Robert replied, 'but you're still overreacting.'

'Overreacting? David's taking Alison to Chania and they'll probably have a romantic lunch somewhere!'

'I imagine Betty asked David to take Alison into Chania and he agreed. He seems the perfect gentleman to me. Men and women can just be friends, you know . . . look at us.'

Eve obviously wasn't cheered up at all by Robert's words, and he felt at a loss how to help her. At least she'd forgotten about the murder for the time being, but he knew it wouldn't be long before she would start thinking about it again. However at least for now she would hopefully be safe.

* * *

Although Eve would rather not have gone to Betty's, once the decision had been made, she just wanted to get there. The day went by slowly, and even though she tried to think about other things, she couldn't. Over and over, Eve wondered if David would be with Alison, and whether her chance with him had completely disappeared. Then she thought about the killer, and whether he or she would be coming and would try to hurt her again.

Robert could see that Eve was restless, so he persuaded her to go to the beach with him. The summer in England hadn't been good, and he was eager for some sun and the sea. Like Eve, he loved the heat, but she wanted to look good for the evening and was worried that the seawater would ruin her hair. However, Robert promised they'd be back by four, giving her plenty of time to get ready.

Eve and Robert were soon lying on the beach, and as she stretched out in the sun, Eve decided it had been a good idea to come after all. She'd look even browner by the evening. She had a lovely white dress that nobody had yet seen, and she could wear it tonight. It was tight-fitting and would show off her figure, while the colour would accentuate her tan.

She smiled, thinking that Alison wasn't nearly as slim or as brown as she was . . . but what if David preferred voluptuous women? She sat up, frowning; she was letting her mind wander again and silly thoughts were entering her head. Swimming always calmed her down, so she got up and went into the sea, letting the warm waters of the Aegean soothe her.

★   ★   ★

It was almost eight and Eve still wasn't ready. Robert, growing impatient, thought that she really was going to too much trouble for this David bloke. It surprised him to see this different side of Eve's character. Ever since he had known her; she had always been completely in control of her own emotions.

'Come on, we'll be late,' he shouted up to her.

'We don't want to be there dead on eight. You know I hate to be the first to arrive anywhere.'

Robert sighed. 'You said it's a ten-minute walk, so we're not going to be that early.'

'Okay I'll be ready in a few minutes,' Eve shouted.

When Eve finally came down the stairs, Robert gasped. Her figure was perfect, her tan was highlighted by her white dress, and her make-up had been immaculately applied. She looked as beautiful as when he had first met her fifteen years ago. She had kept her figure, and despite her constant quest for a tan, she didn't have many wrinkles. He knew she spent a fortune on creams and moisturisers and it had definitely paid off.

* * *

As they approached Betty and Don's house, Robert and Eve could hear people talking, and she was relieved that they weren't the first to arrive after all. As they went in, everyone turned and looked, and Eve smiled graciously at her audience. She knew she looked good this evening and could tell that everyone was impressed. In addition, Robert was handsome and charming, and they made an outstanding couple. David was turning out to be hard work, and she wished she could stop thinking about him so much.

Eve glanced around the room and saw Betty walking towards her, frowning. Then, realising that Eve was looking at her, her hostess attempted to smile.

'Lovely to see you,' she gushed. 'Don will get you a drink.'

'Thank you. We've been looking forward to this all day,' Eve replied, giving her most gracious smile.

She was pleased now that she'd spent so much time getting ready — if nothing else, Betty was clearly jealous of her looks.

Eve then spotted David and Alison

talking quietly together in a corner. She knew she outshone Alison, but would it make any difference? David looked in her direction, but Eve couldn't tell what he was thinking.

'Just as I thought,' Eve said to Robert despondently. 'David's here with Alison.'

'For goodness' sake, Eve, be positive,' Robert said sternly. 'This isn't the Eve I know. You always go for what you want, so get in there and do something about it.'

Robert was right yet again. She never gave up on anything without a fight — but first she needed a drink. Don seemed to be taking his time getting it, but then she shivered, remembering that someone had tampered with her drink at her parly. Although she felt instinctively she could trust Don, she was still nervous after the attempt on her life, and decided to get her own glass of wine.

Returning from the kitchen and taking a long sip, she went over to talk to David and Alison.

'Hello,' she said lightly. 'What a lovely gathering, isn't it? Mind you, after what happened at my party, I'm keeping a tight hold of my drink this time.'

'I'm sure no one will try to poison you again,' David said.

'Probably not, but you can't be too careful.'

Betty watched Eve talking to David. He had been getting on famously with Alison, and she wasn't going to let Eve ruin what could be a wonderful relationship. Where was Robert? He was extremely good-looking and was, in her eyes, much more suitable for Eve. Betty thought with disgust of how superficial and wrapped up in themselves Eve and Robert were. She decided to simply walk over and interrupt their conversation.

'Eve, have you heard? The British police are coming over,' she announced. 'It seems that John did have a family in England after all and they want something done.'

'The British police!' Eve exclaimed. 'I expect they'll want to talk to me after

159

what happened. I could be on TV!'

David stared at Eve. She looked more beautiful tonight than he'd ever seen her, but she was back to her self-centred ways.

'Really, Eve!' Betty continued. 'I would have thought it was more important for them to find out who killed John.'

'Well, yes ... yes, of course it is. Although I don't know what you're getting so worked up about, Betty-you've always made it quite clear that you never liked him.'

'Now, don't be silly,' Alison said quickly, hoping to avoid a confrontation. 'This is a party and we should be enjoying ourselves. Come on, you two, make friends.'

Eve wondered why Alison had to interfere. It had nothing to do with her. Still, two could play that game.

'You're quite right, Alison,' she replied. 'Betty and I shouldn't fight. We've been getting on pretty well lately, haven't we?'

160

Eve smiled sweetly at Betty, and although she knew neither of them was being sincere, Betty smiled back.

'Yes, we have. And you're right, Eve, there was no love lost between John and me, but I was hoping that if they could solve his murder, the situation regarding our houses, might be closer to being resolved. I keep going in to his office, but the girl there says that nothing can be done yet.'

'Yes,' Annie agreed, having just joined the group. 'I've been in too. We really need that patio finished before the winter sets in. If we get a lot of rain, not much will get done.'

Robert came over with a plate of sandwiches and put his other arm around Eve. He hadn't meant anything by it, but he quickly realised that perhaps it gave David the wrong idea.

Betty, however, smiled, thinking that everything was finally going the way she wanted.

David was confused about Eve and Robert. How on earth had this situation

161

come about? He knew he had been moving slowly with Eve, but he'd thought she liked him, and yet now everything seemed to have changed.

Eve must have invited Robert to Crete a little while ago, he reasoned, so why was she flirting with me when she first arrived? And if she's interested in Robert, why is she so angry about me spending time with Alison?

David couldn't understand any of it. The stupid thing was that he only liked Alison as a friend, and knew the feeling was mutual. He had been interested in her last year, but not now . . . not since Eve had captured his heart.

Perhaps his feelings for Alison would return. After all, she was very attractive and was also a much less complicated person than Eve. But the more he thought about it, the more he wanted Eve and nobody else.

'Come on, everyone's dancing outside. We were always good on the dance floor together,' Robert said, taking Eve's arm.

Eve glanced at David. He had been looking at her, but he quickly averted his eyes. Eve felt truly miserable, but tried to hide her true emotions.

'That would be lovely, Robert. It's been a long time since I've hit the dance floor.'

'I think we should dance too, Alison,' David said, kissing her lightly on her cheek.

Betty watched the two couples go outside and smiled. This was just what she had wanted.

But Annie felt that the situation wouldn't end well. 'I don't know what's going on with David and Eve,' she said to her husband. 'Neither of them is happy, but they're both too stubborn to back down and have got themselves in a right old mess. I think they need to have their heads knocked together.'

'Yes, you're right. I think both of them have got the wrong idea about the other. Perhaps we should engineer a private meeting between the two of them? They need to sort things out before it's too late.'

'What a good idea. Meanwhile, about a dance, husband? — I don't think we're quite too old yet, are we?' she smiled.

Pete smiled and took his wife in his arms.

Betty meanwhile, watched contentedly, feeling that her party was turning out to be a great success. As she swayed to the music, she felt a tap on her shoulder and smiled as she saw Jan from The Black Cat.

However, the smile soon left her face and tears sprang to her eyes. Wiping them away, she reached for her CD player and switched off the music. Everybody turned and looked at her.

Eve started shivering, feeling that something was terribly wrong. She didn't know what it was, but she had a sudden sense of foreboding.

'I'm sorry to spoil the party.' Betty started to speak, her voice trembling.

'But I have some very sad news . . . Laura is dead . . . she was shot and has been found in an olive grove just outside the village.'

11

Eve wasn't able to sleep that night. After Betty had told everyone that Laura had been murdered, the party was all but over. The guests were stunned.

Finally, Jan had broken the silence. One of John's former workmen had come into The Black Cat earlier and had told Ken what had happened, also saying that Yiannis had been taken into police custody.

None of the guests seemed surprised that Yiannis had been arrested, and Eve had felt angry with them. She had warned them that Laura could be in danger, but they had ignored her worries, saying they couldn't do anything.

But then she hadn't helped Laura herself, either, had she?

Eve hadn't wanted to stay at Betty's

after the announcement, and she had left soon afterwards with Robert. They had a drink when they got home, but she hadn't felt like talking, so both had gone to bed early. Robert knew Eve well enough to understand when she wanted time on her own to think.

David had watched Eve leave the party without saying goodbye to him, and he was disappointed for a second night in a row. He had thought — hoped, he supposed — that she might have come to talk to him after hearing about Laura's death, but instead she had stuck close to Robert.

Why was he so jealous? Could it be that he was actually falling in love with Eve? This was the sort of complication he really didn't need.

★   ★   ★

Eve tossed and turned in bed and eventually dozed off, but it wasn't long before she woke up again. Her short sleep had nevertheless given her a new perspective on the case.

Was it really Yiannis who had shot Laura? she mused. She was sure he had hit her, and Eve could have imagined Yiannis perhaps hitting her too hard, resulting in accidental death, but shooting would need to have been premeditated and that didn't seem likely.

There had been two murders committed in a small area in a short space of time. It seemed likely to her that the killer was the same person . . . which meant that, if it was Yiannis, then his brother had lied to give him an alibi.

It would also mean that Yiannis had poisoned her — and Eve really didn't think he would use arsenic, reasoning that poison was more of a woman's choice as a murder weapon.

And last, but not least, why would Yiannis kill Laura? It seemed extreme, even if he did think that she had been flirting with other men.

Perhaps Laura knew something about

Yiannis and had threatened to go to the police?

But what if it wasn't Yiannis at all? Perhaps Laura had known who really murdered John — and the killer had decided to act to shut her up.

Eve's head started to hurt. This was getting too complicated and should be best left to the police — but they hadn't got anywhere with John's murder up to now.

She closed her eyes, but all she could she was Laura's sad face and tears welled up once again.

This whole situation just wasn't fair. No, she couldn't give up now. She might not have liked John much, but Laura definitely deserved justice.

*   *   *

Late the following morning. Eve and Robert strolled down to the beach. Eve had her sunglasses on; her eyes looked puffy both from crying and from too little sleep.

169

Robert felt deeply for her. He knew she had warned everybody that Laura was heading for disaster, and that nobody, including herself, had done anything about it. But there again, his logical mind argued, what could anyone have done if Laura continually refused to help herself?

Eve kept thinking of how happy Laura used to be and how she had loved her job, but how miserable she had been during the course of this last year. Why had she stayed with a man who obviously had no respect for her?

Still, after thinking about it all night, Eve had arrived at the conclusion that it wasn't Yiannis who had killed his girlfriend. If it had been him, he would have covered his tracks. He was much too intelligent not to have done so.

As Eve and Robert walked past Hari's, they saw the crowd from last night sitting together. They were all looking very sombre.

'Eve, Robert, come and join us,' Annie called out.

Eve still didn't feel like talking, but she thought it might be useful to know what they were all thinking, so they went over and sat with the group. As well as Annie and Pete, Betty, Don, David, Alison and Phyllis were there. Eve was too upset to even care that Alison and David were sitting next to each other.

'Well,' Betty said. 'It's all very sad, isn't it? Laura was such a sweet girl. I hope they put Yiannis away for a long time.'

'If it really was Yiannis who killed Laura, that is,' Eve returned sharply.

'What do you mean?' Betty challenged her. 'Do you think you know better than the police? After all, he was taken into custody last night.'

Betty glared at Eve, but Eve simply shook her head.

'Don't you think it's a bit of a coincidence?' she replied. 'There have been two murders in a tiny village in the space of just a few days, plus I've been poisoned. It's pretty likely that they've all been committed by the same person, yet Yiannis has an alibi for the first murder and has been cleared of poisoning me.'

'Really? Then why ever would someone else murder Laura?' Betty asked snidely.

'Well,' continued Eve, 'perhaps she discovered who it was who murdered John and poisoned me. There's more than one possibility, after all.'

'I think you have an overactive imagination,' Betty remarked sourly.

'Now, come on, you two, this really isn't the time to argue . . . please,' Annie urged.

The kindly woman looked as if she were close to tears. Eve got up, went across and hugged her.

'I'm sorry, Annie. I haven't had much sleep. It's all been too upsetting,' she explained to her friend.

'Here's the wine,' Pete interrupted. 'Let's drink to Laura's memory.'

They all sipped their wine quietly. David watched Eve, but she avoided his gaze. Why wouldn't she look at him, let alone talk to him? They needed to sort things out between them before it was too late.

'Oh, by the way,' Annie finally said, breaking the sombre silence. 'The British police have arrived.'

'Already?' Eve said, coming alive again. 'I'd better make myself presentable for my interview, then!'

'I don't know why you always think *you're* so important,' Betty snapped. 'Why would they want to talk to you first?'

'Well, because somebody tried to kill me. I think that's reason enough, don't you?'

With that remark, Eve got up, took a few euros out of her purse for her share of the wine and put it on the table, then left the taverna quickly, with Robert in tow.

David watched her, dumbfounded. She hadn't once looked at him. Perhaps he should turn his attentions towards Alison after all?

But he simply wasn't attracted to her, he wasn't interested in having a fling — and in any case she would be heading home in a few days' time.

He had been alone before, and he could be again. Life had certainly been less difficult then . . . but did he really want to return to what would now seem a thoroughly dull and boring existence?

12

The British police were giving Eve a hard time. 'You should leave the investigating to the experts,' one of them said.

Eve hated being told off and gave him a severe look. 'Well, the Greek police haven't got very far in finding John's killer — or the person who poisoned me,' she retorted. 'First of all they thought it was a robbery that had gone wrong, and it wasn't until I was poisoned that they thought it could have been murder.

'And then there's Laura. They've arrested Yiannis Neonaki, but it might not have been him at all. It could have been the same person who committed both murders and poisoned me. I just don't think they're looking into all the possibilities.'

'You really are asking for trouble,

Miss Masters,' the police officer replied sharply. 'You might not be so lucky next time and could end up dead. You're asking too many questions and obviously the murderer doesn't like it.'

Bill Holt generally didn't like amateur detectives, believing they hindered investigations and often put themselves in danger. Mind you, this woman wasn't like most of the nosey parkers he had met. She was stunningly good-looking and seemed intelligent enough. He thought she had probably got involved because she enjoyed being in the limelight. Eve was now looking upset and Bill felt slightly guilty. After all, she had been poisoned and the revelation must have frightened her.

'Look, I'm just saying these things for your own good,' he said gently. 'Someone did try to hurt you and they could make another attempt on your life.'

Eve smiled sweetly, thinking that perhaps she should try charming him. It couldn't do any harm. 'I'm sorry. I know it was stupid of me. I've hardly interfered at all since I was poisoned.'

'Good. I'm pleased to hear it. You're lucky to be alive.'

'Have you any leads on who tried to kill me?' Eve continued. 'I'm not meddling, honestly. It's just — well, I probably know the person who did this. I could be bumping into them every day.'

'We're doing our best to help. Unfortunately, the Greek police don't seem to be able to pin it on anyone at your party, but it must have been someone who was there. We've started interviewing everyone ourselves. You're right, the chances are that it was the same person who killed John. But it does seem to be Yiannis who killed his girlfriend, Laura.'

'But don't you think he would have made sure he had an alibi?' Eve persisted. 'He's much too clever to have the blame fall on him.'

As soon as she had spoken, Eve wished she hadn't. Although she still thought there was a good chance Yiannis hadn't killed Laura, it occurred to her that it would have been better to keep her mouth shut.

Bill scrutinised Eve and knew then that she hadn't really given up trying to solve the murders. However, there was nothing he could do except warn her against the possible consequences of meddling. He hoped that the next time he saw her wasn't in the hospital — or worse still, at the morgue.

'I hear you have a friend staying,' Bill commented as they walked to the door. 'It's quite a good idea to have someone here with you.'

Eve stared at him and suddenly felt sick. The police thought she was still in danger! One brush with death was enough, so perhaps she really should stop her hunt for the killer.

'We'll be on our way now,' Bill said. 'Just be careful.'

As Eve let Bill and the other police officer out, she called to Portia. She felt vulnerable and didn't want to be alone.

Robert had gone down to the beach, determined to go back to England with the perfect tan.

Sitting on the sofa, Eve wished again that her own furniture would arrive from England. This settee wasn't comfortable at all. But still, Eve hugged her dog and closed her eyes, soon drifting off to sleep.

* * *

Half an hour later, somebody shook her shoulder to wake her. She sprang up nervously, her body defensive.

'Sorry! I hope I didn't scare you,' Robert said.

'It's okay. I'm just a bit on edge. The British police still think I'm in danger and told me to stop looking for the killer. I suppose they're right. Anyway, I thought you were spending the whole day on the beach.'

'I was, but I felt a bit selfish leaving you here on your own. How about going into Chania to look for that car

179

you want to buy? That should take your mind off the murders.'

'Are you sure you don't mind? I'd love that,' Eve enthused.

She had told Robert to go to the beach, but she was relieved that she didn't have to spend the day alone and was also excited about looking for a new car. She quite fancied a little sporty model, despite the country roads not really being built for one. There was still the highway after all.

'Come on, then — go and get ready quickly before I change my mind.' Robert laughed at her eagerness.

* * *

Ten minutes later, they were sitting in a very hot car. Eve switched on the air conditioning, deciding that she would have climate control in her new car. It was far better in this heat.

They started meandering along the narrow and winding country lanes and Eve's thoughts drifted.

But it wasn't long before she realised she was going too fast for the state of the roads, and pressed the brake pedal.

Nothing happened.

'Slow down, Eve,' Robert suggested.

'I'm trying,' Eve almost yelled. 'The brakes aren't working.'

Eve pumped the brake pedal, but still nothing happened and the car was beginning to pick up speed, going seriously too fast. Eve could see there was a truck in front of her now and she had no idea what to do. She pulled up the handbrake, but the car was going too fast now and carried on moving.

'Turn into that field, Eve!' Robert shouted.

Eve did as she was told and the car bumped along in the field, with Eve and Robert being thrown up and down. She knew she'd have bruises all over, but that was the least of her worries at the moment.

Finally they heard a bang as the car hit what they thought was a rock, and finally it stopped. Both Eve and Robert sat for several minutes, breathing heavily, without saying a word.

Eventually Robert asked, 'Are you okay?'

'We were nearly killed! How on earth did this happen? I would have thought that the hire car company checked their cars for brake faults.'

'Yes, so would I,' Robert agreed. 'This is looking pretty suspicious to me.'

'Suspicious? Oh! — do you think somebody deliberately sabotaged my car?'

'I don't know, Eve, but it is a possibility.'

'Yes! You're right. Where's that card Bill Holt gave me? I'm phoning him up right now.'

* * *

Within half an hour, Bill Holt had arrived.

'I told you,' he said, staring directly at Eve. 'Interfering would lead to more trouble.'

182

'I promised I wouldn't interfere any more and I haven't! I'm afraid I can't take back what I did before that promise,' Eve remarked stubbornly.

Bill tried to stop a smile appearing on his face. Eve was not only attractive, but she was sharp as well.

'So,' she continued, 'you think somebody may have tampered with my car?'

'Well, it's a distinct possibility. I presume you think so too, and that's why you called me?'

'Yes, it was . . . and Robert agrees.'

As they talked, the Greek police drove up, followed by an ambulance. Eve and Robert were checked over, but their injuries were superficial and they didn't need to go to hospital.

Eve breathed a sigh of relief, one hospital stay having been quite enough for her in such a short space of time. After being questioned briefly by the Greek police, Bill Holt gave Eve and Robert a lift home.

'We'll arrange for the car to be towed

away and checked,' he said. 'Then we'll know if something's been tampered with. I hope you've had your final warning, Eve. Stop investigating.'

'I will, I promise.'

Robert looked at her, and although she looked terrified now, he knew she would soon snap out of it and be back on the trail of the killer again. He wished he could stay on Crete and keep an eye on her, but he had a TV part to get back to next week.

Eve knew Bill was right, but if the killer remained free, she'd never be safe. She had to do something — but she would just have to be more discreet about it.

13

Eve sat outside on her patio sipping a cup of hot, sweet tea. Robert had suggested calling Annie, but at the moment she didn't want to talk to anybody about what had happened.

She was certain that word would get around quickly enough. It always did. Anyway, she wanted to wait and see what Bill found out first before she spoke to her friends. He said he'd come and see her as soon as he had any news.

'I don't mind if you go back to the beach, Robert. I really don't,' she said.

He had come to Crete to check up on her, but he deserved to have a bit of a holiday as well.

'Don't be silly, Eve. After what we've been through today, I'm not really bothered. There's always tomorrow. I'll pop down to the shops though if you like. We're short of a few things.'

'Yes, please. I don't feel like going out again.'

After Robert had left, Eve closed her eyes and soon drifted off into an uneasy sleep, but it wasn't long before a loud knock at the door woke her. Startled, she jumped up, and walking towards the door, wondered whether she would ever feel safe again.

'Who is it?' she called out.

'It's me — David.'

Eve wondered what he wanted. She had put him to the back of her mind since Laura's death.

'Good morning, David,' she said politely, opening the door. 'What can I do for you?'

David's heart sank. She was distant, and he immediately felt that there was no hope for them. He wished he could turn the clock back and see what he had done wrong, if anything. Was it just Alison?

Earlier he had convinced himself that he could get back to life without Eve, but it was turning out to be more difficult than he had imagined. Even though Eve could be frustrating and unpredictable, she was undeniably passionate and there was rarely a dull moment with her.

'I just heard what happened with your car,' he explained. 'I came to see how you were.'

Eve felt her heart beat faster. Perhaps he did still care for her? But then she quashed the thought.

'Come in,' she said. 'Yes, it was very scary. The brakes on the car failed. Bill Holt, the policeman from England, thinks it might have been done deliberately and the garage is checking the car now. How did you find out about it so quickly?'

'I was passing the garage and saw Bill. It looked like your hire car so I stopped and asked him. All he said was that you were involved in an accident.' David almost reached out for her, then checked his impulse. 'Eve — you could have been killed.'

'Yes, we were very lucky.'

David felt miserable again. He should have known Robert would have been with her. He needed to broach the subject and ask her what was going on between her and Robert, but he was scared of having all his dreams shattered.

'Would you like a coffee?' Eve asked. She expected him to refuse, but he said he'd love one. She had thought he wouldn't want to spend time with her and would want to rush back to Alison, but he seemed reluctant to leave and she felt happy again for the first time in days.

⋆ ⋆ ⋆

A few minutes later, they were sitting on the patio drinking their coffee with Portia lying contentedly at Eve's feet.

'That dog is getting spoilt, you know,' David remarked with an indulgent smile.

'She deserves it,' Eve returned. 'She's a great dog.'

'Yes — she's lucky to have you.'

'Actually, you know, I think I'm the one who's lucky to have her,' Eve returned. 'She's become a great companion.'

She smiled and stroked Portia's velvety head. She'd missed seeing David like this, and heartily wished that Alison and Robert would hurry up and go back to England — but perhaps it was already too late for their relationship.

'Hi, I'm back!' Robert called out, coming onto the patio. 'I bumped into Annie. News has already got around the village about our accident, I'm afraid . . . oh, hi, David. I suppose you've heard too? Eve was absolutely brilliant stopping the car. A real heroine.'

'I'm sure she was,' David answered despondently, feeling that his chance for a private chat with Eve had vanished. 'Oh well, I'd better get going, I suppose.' He got up to leave.

'Oh, there's no need to rush off,' Eve

189

said quickly, wanting him to stay.

'I have to meet Alison and take her to see the Roman ruins at Aptera, so I'd better be off, I'm afraid. Thanks very much for the coffee.'

With that, David left and Eve wondered bleakly whether the day could get any worse.

'Well, thanks very much,' she muttered to Robert once David had gone out of earshot. 'You've really gone and frightened him away now.'

'Sorry — I didn't mean to.' Robert shrugged apologetically, surprised at her reaction.

'I know you didn't . . . I'm sorry,' Eve said more gently. 'I'm just a bit cranky. It's been some day.'

'Yes, it has,' replied Robert emphatically. 'Well, I think I'll go and make us some lunch. We'll have a glass of wine and just relax in the sun here. What do you say?'

'That sounds good,' Eve replied gratefully.

She got up from her chair and lay

down on a sun bed. There was no point worrying about David now. Alison and Robert would be gone soon; then she would be able to talk to him quietly, without interruption, and they could finally get everything out in the open.

*   *   *

The afternoon went by quickly and Eve's thoughts gradually became calmer. As the temperature started to drop, she had just decided to take Portia for a walk when Bill Holt arrived.

'Good evening,' she greeted him. 'I think everyone in the village already knows what happened this morning.'

'Yes,' he replied. 'News certainly travels quickly around here, doesn't it? I do hope you eventually manage to settle on Crete, Eve — but if you do, I don't think you'll be able to keep many secrets.' He laughed.

'No.' She grinned, but then became more serious. 'Any news about the car?'

Robert came into the room and

stood expectantly behind Eve, his hands resting reassuringly on her shoulders.

Bill grimaced. 'I'm afraid the news isn't good. The hydraulic brake line on the car was severed, which means that it was definitely done deliberately.' He paused as Eve gasped, and went on, 'This development therefore rules Yiannis out as he's currently in jail. It now seems highly unlikely that he was involved in John's murder at all — or in the previous attempt on your life.'

'So it's just Laura's murder, then?'

'That's debatable now as well.'

'Really?' Eve exclaimed, her eyes flashing. 'I knew it!'

'Calm down,' Bill said. 'Basically, the bullet used to kill Laura didn't come from either of the guns Yiannis has, but from the type of gun that was stolen from John's house. That gun still hasn't been found. Apparently, the Greek police are releasing Yiannis on bail.'

Eve couldn't hide her excitement.

'Eve,' Bill addressed her gravely. 'I really must warn you not to continue meddling. There have already been two attempts on your life and while you've escaped both of them, you may not be so lucky next time. We'll have to go back to England soon, so this investigation will be left in the hands of the local police.'

'I promise I'll be careful,' Eve assured him.

Bill shook his head, knowing there was nothing else he could do if Eve was determined to carry on looking for the killer.

14

The following day, Eve decided to go to the ladies' coffee morning at The Black Cat. Annie had phoned her the previous evening to see how she was after the car incident and had suggested she came down for coffee the next day. Eve didn't really want to see Betty, but she was interested to find out whether any of them had changed their minds about who had committed the murders after what had happened to her.

'Good morning, everybody,' Eve said as she arrived at the bar. 'Hope you don't mind me joining you.'

'I'm pleased you could make it,' Annie replied, signalling Ken for more coffee. 'We were all concerned about you. It must have been terrifying being in a car that wouldn't stop! I'm sure I would have just panicked and not been able to do anything.'

'It was frightening, but I feel all right now. I'm just a bit sore and bruised, that's all.'

Eve didn't think Betty was particularly pleased to see her, but that didn't surprise her at all.

Alison and Phyllis both smiled. 'Pleased to see you out and about,' Alison said. 'What an awful experience.'

'Yes,' Phyllis agreed. 'Somebody certainly wants you dead.'

'Really, Phyllis!' Betty remarked. 'Eve doesn't need to be reminded about it! Anyway, this puts a whole new perspective on everything. Never let it be said that I don't give credit where credit's due, and it seems that you could have been right all along, Eve — Yiannis might not have killed Laura after all.'

'So who do you think it could have been?' Eve asked Betty, curious to know her opinion.

'Well, I reckon one of John's workmen killed him. Laura found out and then he killed her. You were asking too many questions, so he tried to kill you.'

Eve thought that very unlikely, but she didn't want to enter into an argument with Betty, who was always convinced that she was right.

'Don't you think it's better if we stopped discussing possible suspects?' Annie remarked. 'It's getting too dangerous. Whoever it was has tried to kill Eve twice already.'

'I agree,' Alison said with feeling. 'He or she will stop at nothing now.'

Eve thought she wasn't going to get much more out of any of them after this and thought she had probably wasted her morning coming to The Black Cat — but nobody had much of a chance to say anything else anyway when there was a loud clatter as an enormous jukebox was brought into the bar.

'My goodness, that's all we need! We won't get a moment's peace with that thing in here,' Betty grumbled when all the noise had died down. 'Must have cost an absolute fortune for something that size.'

'I thought you said he was having problems paying his bills with the new property tax having come in?' Phyllis remarked.

'I did,' Betty replied. 'Strange . . . perhaps he got the jukebox on credit? Though why would he want to?'

'I heard his uncle back in England died recently and left him a bit of money,' Annie replied.

Or he could have hit John over the head and stolen the money out of his cashbox, thought Eve darkly.

She had ruled Ken out as a suspect in John's murder a long time ago, but he was now back as a possibility. She liked Ken and he didn't seem like a murderer — but then the most unlikely people turned out to be killers.

Why, though, would he kill Laura? It could only be because she had seen or heard something. Everything always came back to poor Laura.

Eve finished her coffee, deciding she

didn't want to spend any more time in The Black Cat after all. Robert only had a few more days on the island and she felt she should be with him.

Anyway, she thought dismissively, she would hardly learn much more from the women. Betty's ideas were never innovative, Phyllis didn't have any thoughts about the murder, Annie thought the whole business should be left to the police and Alison was an outsider.

* * *

Eve and Robert avoided The Black Cat for the rest of his stay. Eve didn't want to see David and Alison together, and instead she spent her time lounging on the beach with Robert. They also did a little sightseeing; she loved visiting the churches and monasteries, finding them peaceful and steeped in history.

Nothing else turned up with regard to the murders, and Eve kept a low profile. Admittedly, the car accident had frightened her — and Robert was in no mood to encourage her to resume her hunt for the killer, his brush with death having shaken him up considerably too.

The British police had gone home, having made little progress as far as Eve and Robert could tell; the Greek police seemed to be no further forward, either. Eve hadn't talked much about it, but Robert knew that although she was nervous now, it wouldn't be long before she would be on the trail of the killer again.

On Robert's last day, Eve decided they should go to the Italian restaurant in Chania for dinner. Eve washed and styled her hair and carefully did her face. She always took enormous care over her appearance, even if she was only going out for fifteen minutes to walk her dog.

'Come on,' Robert shouted up the stairs. 'The taxi will be here in a minute.'

The car hire firm had given Eve

another car, but she had decided they would take a cab into town so that they could both have a drink or two; she was looking forward to a decent bottle of wine. The local stuff was usually okay, but it could sometimes be a bit rough.

As Eve came down the stairs in white cropped trousers and a jade green beaded tunic, Robert thought how beautiful she was — but her eyes looked sad. He did hope things would work out for her; she deserved some happiness. He knew how she must be feeling; he'd been single for too long as well.

Alison was a highly attractive woman, he mused, and she didn't live too far away from him in London. Why on earth hadn't he asked for her phone number?

★ ★ ★

The taxi dropped Eve and Robert off near Chania harbour. The harbour was beautiful at night and there were still tourists milling about. Eve liked it when the place was busy, and decided they would have a short walk before dinner to soak up the atmosphere. When she had come house-hunting in the winter, it had been much quieter, although it livened up on Friday and Saturday nights. However, it didn't start getting hectic until late, and Eve still thought it strange that the Greeks often sat down to eat dinner at eleven or even midnight, thinking that this was surely a recipe for indigestion.

Robert liked Chania as well. Crete had been ruled by many different powers through the centuries and their influence was evident in Chania, from the houses in the old town and in the harbour to the enormous shipyard on the waterfront. The Mosque of the Janisseries, situated among the cafés in the harbour, was a reminder of when the Turks ruled Crete.

Robert had decided he was going to read more about the history of the island. He wasn't an avid reader, but he was becoming fascinated by Crete's past.

He hoped Eve didn't want to go for a long walk. As usual, he was hungry. He'd always had a healthy appetite and never seemed to put on weight. But as they walked by the tavernas and bars, Eve glanced critically at him and thought he seemed a little heavier since he'd arrived on Crete. He'd have to go to the gym more regularly once he got back home.

'Let's go and eat,' Eve finally said. 'I'm starting to feel hungry; the walk must have built up my appetite.'

'Great. I'm starving.'

Eve smiled. Robert had demolished a cooked breakfast and two sandwiches for lunch, not to mention cake and coffee.

As they approached the restaurant, they heard a voice calling.

'Hello! How lovely to see you.'

Eve looked round and, with a sinking feeling, saw Alison waving to them.

Standing with her were David, Betty and Don.

'We're still waiting to be seated,' Alison remarked. 'Why don't we get a table for six?'

'They might want to be on their own,' Betty said quickly.

'No,' Robert interjected. 'We'd love to join you. We've had lots of time alone. It would be really nice to spend my last night with you all.'

'It's your last night?' Alison asked. 'Mine too. I'm on the Monarch flight back to Gatwick tomorrow.'

'Really? Same as me — what a coincidence. Perhaps we can keep each other company?'

'That would be great. I always seem to end up sitting next to some really strange person when I travel on my own.'

'Tomorrow won't be any exception, then!' Eve joked.

Everybody laughed apart from Betty. She had been imagining David and Alison's future together, but it now seemed as if her hard work had been a waste of time. She'd been delighted when David had said he was going to England to see his publisher in the autumn, and Alison had invited him to visit her. Why did Robert have to get involved?

A waiter approached. 'Your table is ready,' he said.

'There are six of us now. Will that be okay?' Alison asked.

'Of course. Come this way.'

Eve didn't want to sit with the group, but she felt trapped. Still, she smiled as she entered the restaurant, thinking how lovely it was. In the local tavernas, customers just sat down wherever they wanted and there were paper cloths on the tables. Here there were proper tablecloths and napkins, and the waiters poured your wine.

Eve's affection for the Greeks came and went, and she was now starting to get homesick again. This restaurant was as good as the ones in London, but such places were few and far between on Crete.

The table was round, and Eve found herself sitting in between Robert and Don, Betty having rushed to the table to make sure Eve didn't get a seat next to David. It had become obvious that the woman intended to do anything in her power to keep them apart, but Eve didn't care any more. The evening was ruined. She hadn't wanted to spend it with the ex-pats and had been looking forward to a quiet dinner with Robert, her old friend, simply enjoying good food and wine.

Now however, she had to watch David and Alison together and put up with Betty's antics. Nothing was going to plan any more and she felt as if other people were trying to run her life.

Then she glanced at Betty's smug face and pulled herself together. This wasn't like her. She didn't usually give in and accept defeat, and at that moment she made a fresh resolve to fight for what she wanted.

Once Robert and Alison had gone home tomorrow, she could explain to David that there had been nothing going on between her and Robert. She also needed to find out from him whether he really had feelings for Alison, or if they were just friends.

'Eve! You're not looking at the menu.' A loud voice broke into her thoughts.

Eve glared. People accused her of being bossy, but she was a mouse compared to Betty!

'That's because I've already decided what to have, Betty,' Eve replied, trying to hold back her anger. 'I've been here a few times, so I know the menu.'

After the way Betty had been treating her, Eve didn't care that she was showing off. The restaurant was expensive and not a place Betty could afford to come to often.

'I'm going to start with the tricolori salad, with a side order of foccacia,' Eve continued. 'Then I'll have the mushroom risotto. It's absolutely delicious.'

'We'll have to make sure that we get

separate bills,' Betty said quickly. 'Only fair if some people have more expensive dishes than others.'

Eve smiled to herself. She didn't expect Betty to pay for any of her food, but thought she'd wind her up anyway.

'Oh,' Eve said, looking surprised. 'Whatever you want. Sorry, I'm not used to this. My friends and I usually just split the bill. It all works out evenly in the long run. But we probably won't be eating out together again, will we, Betty?'

Betty said nothing, thinking Eve was making a fool of her.

'Look,' Alison said. 'I agree with Eve. 'It'll only complicate matters if we ask for separate bills. We'll split it four by two. Eve's having the vegetarian options which are a bit cheaper than the meat dishes, so she won't be gaining anything. Anyway, I'm treating you and Don to thank you for having me to stay.'

Betty admired Alison's generosity, but she wasn't happy that Eve had seemingly won this battle.

With the food ordered and the wine poured, however, everybody started to relax.

Eve observed how quiet Don was. He seemed to be a shy man, but then she imagined he was rarely given the chance to talk. She then turned her attention to Alison, asking her about her visit and how she had enjoyed her time on Crete. Alison informed her that she had loved her holiday, but she was looking forward to getting back to London. The two women dominated the conversation, talking about life in the metropolis.

'I could never leave London,' Alison stated. 'I've had a great time here, but I do miss the excitement of a big city.'

Eve glanced at David and thought that he seemed disappointed. Now was the time to go in for the kill and make him see that Alison wasn't the woman for him. She was completely unsuitable and Eve wanted to prove it.

'Oh, I miss London, too,' Eve said,

'but surprisingly, it's taken me no time at all to settle here. I plan to go back to England a couple of times a year to get that kick — you know, to go to the theatre, museums and art galleries, meet friends, and so on. Then I'll be able to enjoy it here the rest of the time. Chania is great,' she went on. 'I aim to come in a lot, but I'm finding that the village is fun too. Everybody is so nice and I've made lots of friends already. It's a real community — and I'm realising that's the one thing which is inevitably missing from life in a big city.'

Glancing at Betty, she was pleased to see a look of anger cloud her face, while David had his eyes fixed on Eve.

Robert simply watched the whole show, knowing perfectly well what Eve was up to. He wouldn't be surprised if she got together with David as soon as he and Alison had left. Perhaps he should help it along a little by flirting with Alison? he wondered. Then he could continue on the plane tomorrow.

It wouldn't be a sacrifice to do this for Eve; Alison was good-looking and smart, and he had already thought that he wouldn't mind getting to know her better.

It was about time he got serious with a woman, he mused. He was over forty and had never been married. Perhaps it was time he settled down.

15

Eve stood in line at the airport with Robert, waiting to check in his luggage. For the most part, she had enjoyed having him to stay. He was probably her only true friend and he knew her better than anyone else, but she could not deny that together with Alison's, his presence had upset her relationship with David. So on balance she didn't mind that he was going home, despite the fact that she was a little scared of being in the house alone.

However, she was optimistic that she might still be able to work things out with David now that they were gone — that was, if he was still interested.

Standing in the long queue of holidaymakers, Eve was quiet, remembering how strange the previous evening had been. Robert had spent most of the remaining time chatting to

Alison, while Betty had desperately tried to bring David into their conversation.

Eve had talked to Don, and had been surprised to discover how interesting he was, having had very little to do with him previously. She had discovered that he liked the theatre and had gone to see plays regularly back in England. However, Betty hadn't shared his interest and he had always gone to watch the performances by himself. He had even dabbled in amateur dramatics, but had been disappointed that his wife had never been curious to see him act.

Eve mused that they must have been in love once, but she saw little sign of that now. Perhaps Betty had been different when they had first met. After all, that was over forty years ago. She wondered why Don stayed with her, but perhaps it was easier to stay than to go, or perhaps they were the type of people who didn't show their affections in public. Who knew what went on behind closed doors?

'Hello!' A breathless voice spoke behind them. Eve and Robert turned to see Alison hauling her suitcase into the queue.

'Hi,' Robert said, smiling warmly. 'We did wait for you at the entrance, but time was getting tight.'

'I'm sorry. David had a flat tyre and he had to change it before we could set off.'

'I wish I'd thought of it earlier — we should have gone in one car,' Robert remarked. 'It would have made more sense.'

Eve could have kicked herself. Why hadn't she thought of that? Then she could have driven back with David and they would have had a chance to talk. What was wrong with her? She had missed the ideal opportunity to be alone with him.

'Where's David now?' Eve asked Alison.

'Parking the car. He dropped me off to save a bit of time.' She paused for a moment as she dug out her passport and tickets. 'It was a good evening last night, wasn't it?' Alison continued. 'The restaurant was absolutely lovely and the food was delicious.'

'Yes, it's my favourite place to eat,' Eve replied.

'I'm pleased you got here before I checked in, Alison,' Robert put in. 'We'll be able to get seats next to each other.'

'Yes,' Alison agreed, smiling. 'I was hoping we could continue our conversation from last night.'

They seemed so at ease with each other and Eve now felt sure that there couldn't have been anything serious going on between Alison and David. Robert had been right; David was just being the perfect gentleman and had been showing Alison around Crete, not courting her. She wished Betty were here now. She would be so mad!

'Hello! I finally managed to get parked.'

Eve turned round, and seeing David, felt herself shiver. She had been acting like a fool this past week, and she scolded herself; she had better get her act together before she frightened him away for good. She didn't want to end up miserable and calculating like Betty, and she certainly wasn't prepared to allow that woman destroy her own happiness.

However she still had a nagging desire to solve the murders, if only to ensure her safety, and she knew David wasn't keen on her carrying on with these plans. She would have to use all her feminine wiles to get him to help her.

'Well done,' Alison was saying to David. 'The traffic, looked really busy out there and I couldn't see any spare places to park. It's not been the best of mornings, has it?'

'No, but we got here on time and that's all that matters,' David replied. He smiled at her. Alison was attractive, generous and always helpful, but she didn't make his heart miss a beat — not like Eve. Seeing her had made him tremble and filled him with anticipation, but he avoided looking into her eyes, afraid that he might not see the same feelings there.

He'd noticed her as he soon as he walked through the airport doors, and she was as beautiful as she had been last night. Why hadn't he suggested they all came to the airport together? Then he could have driven her home and they could have talked without anyone else interfering.

Betty had been so keen to say her goodbyes to Robert and Eve after dinner that he hadn't had a chance to think about today's travel arrangements. Why did that woman have to interfere all the time? He was really beginning to dislike her.

Alison watched Eve and David. It was obvious that they had strong feelings for each other. She knew that for some reason Betty didn't want them to be together, but it was nothing to do with her. She had known her aunt had an unfortunate tendency to interfere continually in other people's lives, but comforted herself with the thought that strong-minded Eve certainly wouldn't put up with it for long.

Alison liked David and she had enjoyed their time together, but she couldn't imagine ever falling in love with him — and she believed he felt the same about her.

But Robert . . . now he was different, he did excite her, especially after the previous evening. He was fun, attractive, intelligent and liked the same things as she did. She was looking forward to sitting with him on the plane and hoped he would ask to see her again in London.

After Robert and Alison had checked in their bags, they said their goodbyes. Robert kissed Eve and David kissed Alison, but they all knew that everything was about to change.

David and Eve watched their friends getting on the escalator. Eve felt a strange sensation of disconnection and new possibilities; she hoped that this was the end of one chapter and the beginning of the next.

'Well, this is rather a weird situation, isn't it? I hate goodbyes and endings,' David remarked.

Eve agreed, hoping that he meant that his relationship with Alison, whatever it had been, had ended. For once, she didn't know what to do next. She didn't want to simply leave everything like this and go home alone to a nearly empty house. She loved her dog, Portia, and was glad every day that she had come into her life, but she wanted so much more.

'So, do you fancy a drink tonight?' David asked nervously.

After what had happened since the arrival of Alison and Robert, he didn't know how Eve felt. He had hoped she would suggest a meeting, but when she hadn't, he decided to make the first move for a change. He wasn't going to let her go without trying to do something.

Betty had caused a lot of damage,

and he had simply gone along with it. It was about time he tried to repair some of the harm that had been done.

'I'd love that,' Eve enthused, much to David's relief. 'But not at The Black Cat. There'll be too many people there that we know. I'd prefer a quiet drink somewhere else.'

'Me too,' David replied. 'Betty might be there, and I've had enough of her for the time being. She was being particularly obnoxious last night.'

Eve hid a smile, pleased that David was finally starting to see Betty for what she really was.

'I know a nice little Greek bar,' he continued. 'I go there sometimes when I want a bit of peace and quiet. It's mainly locals who go there, not foreigners. I hope that won't be a problem for you?'

David knew Eve was taking a while to settle into the Greek way of life, so was surprised by her reply.

'Of course not.' Her eyes sparkled. 'I'd love to try it.'

'I'll pick you up at eight then,' he answered happily.

* * *

Eve smiled to herself on the return journey. Things were getting back on track. Once she reached home, however, she started to feel nervous about spending time alone with David. In the end, she decided to go to the beach for the rest of the day, thinking that relaxing would get her into the right frame of mind for the evening. She was thinking of this as their first proper date and she didn't want to do anything to spoil it.

After soaking up the sun for a couple of hours, Eve walked home. Yawning as she sat down in the kitchen, she thought that perhaps she should have a siesta. It was the Greek way of doing things, after all and Eve didn't feel guilty about going to bed during the day. It was five o'clock and David wasn't picking her up until eight, so she could have an hour or so in bed. She undressed and a couple of minutes later was sound asleep.

* * *

Eve woke with a start, and for a moment didn't know where she was, until she looked at her clock and saw that it was seven fifteen. 'Oh no!' she exclaimed. 'I'll never be ready in time!'

Leaping out of bed, she shot into the shower. A few minutes later, she was out and attempting to style her hair, but it wouldn't do what she wanted. She threw clothes all over the bed, unable to decide what to wear.

But when she opened the door to David a little later, he gasped. She looked gorgeous, and he couldn't wait to spend the evening with her. At last they could sort out what had happened this past week.

It didn't take long to get to the bar, but Eve was a little wary when she saw the place. It looked like a kafenion, a traditional coffee shop where older men gathered without their wives — and there were in fact a few elderly men sitting outdoors — but when they went in, Eve saw that the interior was quite trendy.

The owner, Demetri, rushed forward to greet David and shook his hand. He smiled at Eve and led them to a table. Eve was impressed that David was being treated as a friend and was surprised at how comfortable she already felt there. Demetri brought them wine and a plate of mezes.

'The mezes are on the house,' David whispered to Eve. 'They always treat me well here.'

It all looked delicious. Eve tasted the dolmades and the little cheese pies, reflecting that she was finally settling on Crete, despite the attempts on her life, the grumpy taxi drivers and the lack of sophistication. Sipping her wine, she started to relax, relieved that they hadn't gone to The Black Cat where they would probably have bumped into the people they knew — she wanted David to herself and tonight was her chance.

Nevertheless, Eve found her thoughts wandering to Robert and how he had got on with Alison on the plane.

'Robert and Alison should be arriving home by now,' David said, almost as if he had been able to read her thoughts.

'Yes. I hope they had a good flight,' Eve murmured, suddenly shy. It was quite out of character for her, but she was afraid of saying the wrong thing and pushing David away again.

'Will you miss him?'

'Sorry,' Eve replied. 'Who?'.

'Robert.'

'Oh-he's a great guy,' Eve replied, 'but we had our chance a long time ago. It's too late for us to be a couple now.'

'Oh — I thought . . . ?'

'No, we're just good friends.'

Eve chose not to elaborate. She'd made it clear she wasn't interested in Robert romantically and it was better that she stopped there before saying the wrong thing.

'And you and Alison . . . ?' she continued, apprehensive as she waited for David's response.

'She's a wonderful girl and we had a great time together . . . '

Eve tried to stop herself from frowning. She didn't like it when he talked affectionately about other women, but she had to know the truth.

'But we don't really have enough in common,' he continued. 'She's more interested in living in the fast lane than I am. And anyway, she won't leave London and I won't leave Crete. Perhaps something will happen between her and Robert. They were getting on well last night, weren't they?'

Eve nodded. She was pleased that he didn't seem particularly interested in Alison, but she knew she wasn't really so very different from Alison and so his objections could equally apply to herself. She also liked the excitement of

London and had often questioned her decision to move to Crete. She adored the long hot summers, but that wasn't the best reason for emigrating. She had considered it was time for a change in her life, but perhaps she should have done something less radical — like moving house within London, or getting a different job.

Things hadn't been dull since she had come to Crete, but village life was generally quiet. She couldn't expect to have this degree of excitement all the time. However, she was wealthy enough to visit England for long weekends whenever she got bored, and could also spend a couple of days in Athens now and then. She imagined there was more to do there, and as the flight from Chania to Athens only took forty-five minutes, she had even thought of going there on a shopping trip for the day.

She knew David enjoyed a peaceful life, but she was an independent woman and needed to have some freedom.

Eve took another sip of wine. It was exciting thinking of a future with David, though. She looked at him and shivered, finding it hard to believe they were sitting here together after everything that had happened recently.

She imagined what Betty would think if she walked into the bar now and saw them together. In a way Eve thought it would be fun to see Betty's reaction, but she was having a great time with David and didn't want the evening to be ruined.

Who knew where this night might lead? They could take a long, romantic walk on the beach holding hands . . . but Eve remembered that she was wearing high heels and would hate walking on the sand in them.

'I think we need more wine,' David commented, interrupting her turbulent thoughts.

'Okay. That would be lovely.'

She wanted the evening to go on for as long as possible, but just as she thought it was turning out to be a perfect date, Eve looked up and her face fell. David was surprised to see her mood change so quickly.

'Oh no,' she muttered despondently. 'That's one person I really don't want to see.'

David sighed, thinking that Betty had walked in. He wasn't looking forward to a confrontation with her. But when he turned, he saw Yiannis. David had never seen him in this bar before; he knew that the Greek tended to go to the more fashionable places in the resorts and in Chania. Why did he have to pick tonight to come here? He would probably remind Eve of her near escapes from death, and also of John and Laura's murders. David had hoped that the car accident had frightened her so much that she had put it all to the back of her mind and had given up searching for the killer.

'Well, look who's here,' Yiannis said, approaching Eve. 'Looks like it wasn't me who poisoned you after all — seeing as someone else tried to kill you while I was in jail.'

'I didn't once say I thought it was you,' Eve answered immediately. 'The police questioned everyone at my party. I would imagine that quite a few people would have told them that you attacked me.'

Yiannis smiled. 'Well, they didn't get anything on me. It must worry you that the person who tried to kill you is still free.'

'I think that's enough, Yiannis,' David said firmly.

Yiannis simply smiled again before moving away, but Eve shivered with fear. Although it seemed Yiannis probably hadn't committed any of the crimes, Eve still didn't like him. There was something extremely unpleasant and creepy about him, and he seemed to enjoy intimidating and frightening her. Seeing him again also reminded her of Laura, about whom he had appeared to show no grief, and she felt tears welling up inside her.

'Hey, are you all right?' David asked gently. 'He's really upset you again, hasn't he?'

'A bit. He's just reminded me of Laura again . . . poor girl . . . '

David took Eve's hand and for a few moments she felt so comfortable sitting with him. As she took another sip of wine, however, she started to feel angry. Memories of both attempts on her life came flooding back, and with them her conviction that she had to find out who had tried to kill her and who killed both John and Laura. She was sure she could still discover who the culprit was, but she had to be discreet.

She glanced at David, believing he would help her even if he thought it wasn't the right thing to do. Of course, he might try to dissuade her, but that was a minor problem. She was sure she could convince him to do almost anything.

David watched Eve, aware that her mind was somewhere else. He had a horrible feeling that she had started to think about solving the murders again. He'd been looking forward to a peaceful and romantic evening, and had even imagined kissing her under the stars, but this dream was now fading rapidly.

'What are you thinking, Eve?' he asked her nervously. He had to know what was going through her mind, even if it wasn't what he wanted to hear.

'I'm sorry, David,' Eve replied. 'I know you're going to be cross with me, but seeing Yiannis again has got me all riled up. After all, somebody killed John and Laura and tried to murder me. So far Yiannis has been the prime suspect, but he's been released and it's very frustrating that the police don't suspect anyone else. I don't suppose you've heard anything recently?'

'Unfortunately, not a lot: I know the British police have gone back home and Betty said the Greek police have got no further evidence, but I expect you know all that.'

'I reckon the police are just giving

up,' Eve declared. 'I bet nothing else is going to be done and the murderer is going to get away with it. I know you're not keen on me doing this, but I don't want to live in fear wondering if someone's going to try to kill me again. I'm sorry, but I can't just sit here without doing anything.'

'Oh Eve — you know it's dangerous to interfere. Look what happened to you last time. If the murderer thinks you're back on his or her trail, they might try to kill you again.'

'I'll be more careful, I promise. But if I don't try, somebody is going to get away with two murders.'

'I dread asking this, but what do you intend to do?'

'I really haven't given it much thought. Believe me, I really had put it all to the back of my mind in recent days.'

Eve paused for a moment. She thought about telling him of her suspicions about Ken, but then decided not to. David had been adamant that

Ken would never have killed John and she did like Ken herself . . . but he did have a motive, so she was going to keep him in mind.

'I think we need to start at the beginning,' she finally resumed. 'We should find out more about John's life. A lot of people disliked him, but we don't really know that much about him. He must have had some friends who can tell us more.'

'I actually don't think he did have many friends. He was obsessed with making money and he was only seen out with business colleagues or potential clients.'

'What about women, then? Did he ever have a girlfriend?'

'Not as far as I know,' David replied. 'But then he could have been discreet.'

David wished heartily that Eve wasn't so keen to carry on with this, but he understood why. If he was honest, he didn't have much faith in the Greek police finding out who had committed the crimes either. They had seemed happy to hand the case over to the British police, but now that they had returned to the UK without finding anything, the case seemed to be more or less closed.

'I have an idea,' Eve said after a few moments, her eyes bright with daring. 'I think we should break into John's house and see if we can find anything!'

'That's crazy, Eve!' David exclaimed. 'What if someone sees us? We could be the ones ending up in prison.'

'Well — if you don't want to help me . . . '

'I didn't say that. I just don't think it's a good idea. I mean, aren't you scared? If we go in daylight, we'll be spotted breaking in. And if we go at night, we'll have to switch the lights on. Somebody will probably see them and call the police.'

'The shutters are all down so nobody will know we're there. We'll take torches and just put them on when we go into the different rooms.'

'But what do you think we might

find? I'm sure the police have looked all over the house.'

'They might have missed something. Come on, it's worth a look. If we don't find anything, I promise I'll give up.'

David found it hard to believe that Eve would really stop investigating, and although he didn't want to get involved, he was worried about her taking such a risk on her own. He didn't know what to do.

Eve could see that he was undecided. She didn't want to scare him away, but she had to find out who had tried to kill her — and she was convinced that it was the same person who had killed John and Laura.

She didn't want to push David away, not when their relationship was getting back on track, and although she was uneasy about breaking into John's house, she simply had to find out who it was. If she had to do it on her own, she would.

'Look,' she said earnestly. 'I know it's a difficult decision to make. We'd be breaking the law, so I don't blame you if you don't want to do it, but I'm going to give it a go. I'll be at John's house tomorrow night at nine. It'll be great if you decide to come, but I won't hold it against you if you don't.'

David stared at Eve. She wasn't being bossy or demanding, but was she trying to manipulate him? Should he agree to go or should he try and dissuade her?

While he was agonising, Eve's mobile rang. Her face registered shock as she gave a series of exclamations and asked the caller if there was anything she could do.

'I can't believe it,' she exclaimed moments later. 'That was Annie. Ken's been knocked down outside the cash and carry in Chania and is in a coma in hospital. It was a hit and run.'

David gasped. 'Oh no, how awful! I hope he's going to be okay. How could someone just drive away?'

'Well . . . they could if it was deliberate.'

David stared at Eve, trying to take in what she was obviously implying.

* * *

Lying in bed later that night. Eve couldn't sleep.

David had kissed her gently when he dropped her off, but both had been preoccupied with the news about Ken. Unwillingly David had agreed with Eve's theory. In the light of recent events, it seemed highly likely that Ken had found out something about the murderer and had been run over deliberately.

Eve tossed and turned in bed, unable to stop thinking. Ken couldn't have been the killer after all. Perhaps Yiannis had been the murderer all along, and had got his brother to tamper with the brakes on her car while he was in jail.

Eve sat up, frightened. The killer had to be stopped — otherwise she would never have a good night's sleep again.

When David had got home, he'd sat

up for a while thinking about Ken and resolved to go and see him in hospital the following morning.

It wasn't until he got into bed that he remembered about Eve's proposed break-in. They had been so wrapped up talking about Ken that they hadn't even mentioned it when he dropped her off at home. Could he really leave her to do it on her own?

16

Eve stood outside John's house at nine o'clock the following evening, wearing a black T-shirt and black trousers, and trembling with both excitement and fear.

However, she knew she hadn't formed a proper plan. How was she going to break into the house? Having spent most of the day thinking about Ken, she hadn't even decided what she was going to do when she got to John's house. David would have come up with an idea, of course ... but he had thought this was crazy and she doubted now that he would turn up.

He might be too busy to come. Annie had phoned her in the afternoon to tell her that because Ken was still in a coma, the men were taking turns running The Black Cat so that Jan could stay with her husband in hospital.

David was bound to offer to help out too.

Eve decided to go to the back of the house and try the door, hoping that the police hadn't bothered locking the house properly — but unfortunately they had.

'Damn,' she said out loud. 'What am I going to do now?'

Perhaps this had been a stupid idea after all. When she had seen Yiannis the previous night, her determination to find the murderer had returned, but now she felt out of her depth and knew David had shown good sense staying at home.

Still, she felt a little let down. This was risky and she needed him; he could at least have phoned to say he wasn't coming.

Unsure of what to do next, Eve looked up at the first floor of the house — and then saw that one of the window shutters was open. Perhaps the police hadn't been as careful as they should have been . . . and maybe the window wasn't locked either.

She imagined it had been the Greek police who had left the shutter open, not the English. Bill Holt wouldn't have been so forgetful. Despite her growing affection for the Greeks, there was still a small part of her that felt that the British perhaps did things a little more efficiently.

'A ladder. I need a ladder,' she said excitedly.

Eve immediately wished she hadn't spoken out loud again, realising that someone could be passing. She knew she wasn't thinking straight — so perhaps it was time to give up. Or maybe she should go home and get the ladder she had in the basement? But she didn't know whether it would be long enough to reach to the first floor window.

She paused for a few moments before deciding to carry on, knowing she wouldn't feel completely safe until the killer was behind bars. Eve wasn't going to give up tonight without trying.

As she turned round, someone touched her on the shoulder. She almost screamed, but then a voice spoke quietly in her ear.

'Some burglar you are,' David murmured, laughing. 'You haven't come prepared at all. Will this help?'

'A key? You have a *key?*'

'I went to feed John's cat when he was away recently, and I still have his key. I should have given it to the police, but I forgot all about it when they were questioning me.'

'Why didn't you tell me this before?' Eve said crossly.

Straight away she regretted speaking so harshly. David had turned up to help her and she already felt safer with him there.

'I'm sorry I snapped,' she said quietly. 'I'm really pleased that you've come. I'm just a bit on edge. Believe it or not, I'm not used to breaking into houses! I do feel much better now that I'm not on my own. By the way, what happened to the cat?'

David smiled. Eve really did have a soft spot for animals.

'Petros took it in. His daughter loves cats.'

Eve hugged David and kissed him softly on the cheek.

She felt soft and warm against him and he forgot her quick temper. Pushing his hands through her hair, he cupped her face gently and kissed her. Eve was caught by surprise and felt her whole body tingle as their lips met. Perhaps they should forget about breaking into John's house? But before she could suggest doing something more romantic, David broke away and spoke.

'Come on. We're here now. Let's go in, if only to put your mind at ease. I doubt if we'll find anything, but it's worth a look.'

David unlocked the door and they entered quietly. Luckily both of them had remembered to bring torches.

'You go upstairs, David,' Eve whispered. 'I'll have a look down here.'

David thought ruefully once more how attractive she was, even when she was breaking the law! In between worrying about whether Ken would recover and working out the rota for The Black Cat with the other ex-pat men, he had been thinking about Eve all day and was glad he'd come along to keep an eye on her. He didn't want her to get into any sort of trouble with the police, and hoped he might be able to prevent her from doing anything too rash.

Ten minutes later, David came back downstairs.

'Couldn't find anything,' he said flatly. 'John's clothes are still in the wardrobes, but there's nothing else around.'

'Not much down here either,' Eve replied despondently.

She opened the last drawer in John's cabinet. Pausing, she took out a pile of papers.

'Oh — look what I've found. It's some paperwork for the houses John was having built. I don't suppose there'll be anything here to help with his murder, but I think I'll take a quick look anyway.' She glanced up, seeking his approval. 'We might discover something useful about what's going on with the unfinished houses. Nobody's been told anything yet. Annie and Betty have both been to the office a few times, but they've just been brushed off. I was going to go in tomorrow — not that I think it will do any good. It's worth flicking through this lot of papers, don't you think?'

'Okay, but be quick. We don't want to stay here any longer than we have to. It would be awful if we were discovered. The police wouldn't be too happy with us being here. They've already given you a telling-off and warned you to keep your nose out of their investigations, remember.'

'I know — I won't be long. There isn't much here, anyway. I think most of his business papers have been taken to the office. They must have missed this batch.'

Eve skimmed through the sheaf of paperwork and then suddenly stopped. David watched her intently reading a small folded piece of paper, waiting until she finished before he spoke.

'What is it?' he asked.

'I don't think the police found this,' she breathed. 'I doubt whether anyone has seen it — otherwise we'd probably have heard all about it.'

'What is it? What did you find?' he asked again.

'You won't believe this, David . . . it's a love letter. From Phyllis — to John.'

'You're right, I don't believe it!' David exclaimed. 'I can't see them having an affair. I've never seen them together- I didn't think they even knew each other. Phyllis and her husband bought their house through another agent.'

'Well, there was definitely something going on between them. Not only that, it seems to have been pretty steamy. I think you should read the letter. I would never have thought Phyllis could have written something like this. And you said she was mourning her husband!'

'I thought she was. He only died just before Christmas. I can't believe she would start up with someone else so soon after his death.'

'Perhaps it wasn't a happy marriage. Or maybe Phyllis and John had started seeing each other before her husband died.'

'No! I can't imagine that,' David said, shaking his head. 'Phyllis and Len appeared very close. They were always together and seemed very much in love. I thought it was quite unusual for a couple that had been married for so long. I think they were about to celebrate their thirty-fifth wedding anniversary.'

'It could have just been for show,' Eve observed. 'People do pretend to have happy marriages when the complete opposite is true. Or perhaps they really were in love, and she found it hard to cope after he died. Maybe she found it impossible being alone and that's what made her turn to another man. She could have rushed into another relationship to get over Len. I know she relies on Betty, but for some women that's not enough. They feel they need a man to protect them.'

David was surprised at how intuitive Eve could be, in contrast to her usual bluntness. She was a complex woman and he was finding it exhilarating discovering new things about her. He didn't care any more that she could be hard work. Relationships never ran smoothly all the time anyway, and he certainly wouldn't want a woman without character. Life had become much more interesting since Eve had moved to Crete, and he didn't feel he'd be able to go back to such a quiet existence again.

But he was nervous about being in John's house for so long. Although he was glad he'd come to help Eve, he had no wish to get into trouble with the police. His Greek wasn't fluent and he didn't want to have to explain what they were doing.

Reluctantly David started to read. He didn't like intruding into the private lives of others and was embarrassed when he saw with how much passion the letter had been written. Phyllis had always appeared shy, but it now seemed there was another side to her altogether. As he continued reading, he realised that she must have been very much in love with John.

'Well, this is certainly an eye-opener,' he commented at last. 'You think you know people, but then they surprise you.'

Eve hoped that he was talking about her as well. She never wanted to be considered boring.

'I think we should get out of here,' David said nervously. 'We've been here a while and we're pushing our luck a bit.'

'But we might find more letters,' Eve protested.

Getting caught up in the moment,

Eve wasn't scared any more, but she saw that David was worried and didn't want to annoy him. He was probably right anyway; perhaps they had been there too long and could be discovered. She didn't relish the thought of spending the night in a Greek jail, and anyway, they had more or less searched the whole house. It was doubtful they would find anything else.

* * *

Eve and David managed to get away from John's home without being seen. Arriving back at her house, David collapsed into a chair. Portia bounded up, ready for a cuddle.

'I think that might have taken a couple of years off my life!' David sighed dramatically. 'I'm sure my blood pressure has gone through the roof.'

'Mine too — but it was exciting, wasn't it? I feel like a real detective now!'

'Or a burglar!' David laughed.

'Let's have a drink,' Eve said, grinning. 'I just fancy a G and T. What about you?'

'A whisky if you've got one. Straight up, no ice. I think I could do with something strong. I'm still shaking.'

Eve got the drinks and opened a packet of nuts. David could see that she was thinking again.

'We have to confront Phyllis,' Eve said after a few moments. 'We have to find out about her relationship with John.'

'How can we do that? Nobody seems to know about it, so it will look suspicious if we start asking questions.'

'You're right. We'll have to be discreet — especially as she could be the murderer.'

'The murderer?' David gasped. 'How did you work that one out? The letter showed she was madly in love with John, so why would she have wanted to kill him? Anyway, she's tiny. I can't see she would have had the strength.'

'Well, we know *she* was in love with

him, but he might not have been as keen on her. Perhaps she wanted it to become more serious and he didn't. Or maybe he dumped her and, she was so angry that she ended up killing him.'

'A crime of passion . . . ' David mused. 'Hmm, I suppose it's a possibility, but I still don't think she would be strong enough. John was a big and powerful man.'

'She wouldn't need that much strength to pick up something and hit him on the head — and he wouldn't have been expecting it,' Eve answered excitedly.

Eve had a vivid imagination, but David enjoyed listening to her. The world she inhabited was so much more exciting than his. While he could imagine anything happening in his books, real life to him was different and more mundane. Eve, however, clearly believed that anything was possible.

'I suppose she could have killed John,' David conceded slowly, 'but I don't know how we can confront her about it.'

Eve thought for a moment. 'We'll have a dinner party!'

'What, just for Phyllis?'

'No, Betty and Don as well. Betty and Phyllis are close so it wouldn't seem strange,' Eve went on excitedly. 'Perhaps Betty knew about the relationship.'

'But you and Betty hate each other. Don't you think she would be a bit suspicious if you invited her for dinner?'

'Possibly . . . but they asked me to their drinks party, so it's simply a return invite. We'll ask Annie and Pete as well to make it a bigger crowd. They're really good friends so it would seem likely that I would invite them. Is this weekend too short notice?'

'Probably not. As you know, most people here don't have a great deal on. Life seems to revolve around The Black Cat.'

'Oh no — I'd forgotten about that. You're all taking turns to run The Black

Cat, aren't you?'

'We are, but for just a couple of days. Jan's sister and nephew are flying over from the UK to run it until Ken is better. That is, presuming . . . '

Eve and David looked at each other. Neither wanted to admit the possibility that Ken might never wake up from his coma.

'Okay,' Eve finally said, breaking the silence. 'I'll ring everybody tomorrow morning. Then I have to plan the menu — it needs to be elegant — I really do have to impress Betty; she's been horrible to me so I don't feel guilty about showing off.'

Eve paused, suddenly wondering whether she had gone too far, speaking in this way about Betty.

'You don't think I'm being too nasty, do you?' she added anxiously.

David smiled. 'Betty has been particularly unpleasant to you recently, so I don't suppose I could really blame you. Just don't go too far.'

'I won't. I promise,' Eve told him.

'Anyway, I'd better go,' he said reluctantly.

David didn't know whether he should kiss Eve again or not. Although he had kissed her earlier, they had just been about to break into John's house and it couldn't have led anywhere. Now it could — and he was scared. After his wife had betrayed him, David had vowed to take any future relationships slowly.

Meanwhile, Eve was hoping that David would kiss her again, and when nothing happened, she wondered whether she should kiss him. She longed to taste his lips on hers once more, but was surprised at how nervous she felt. She didn't want David to feel that things were moving too quickly, and was desperate for him not to run away. It wasn't even just because she wanted him — her practical brain reminded her that she also needed his help in solving the murder, and he had to be at the dinner party!

She was aware that she had kept putting off their romance, but she told herself that she needed to find John's killer first. However, deep down she was unsure of herself. Despite being in her early forties, David was the first man she had ever met with whom she could imagine a future — and the prospect actually frightened her.

They both got up, and Eve walked David to the door. Neither said anything, but after she had opened the door, she kissed him lightly on the cheek.

'I'll let you know if it's all systems go for the dinner party. Then perhaps you could come round early on the day so we can discuss strategies?'

'Yes, of course,' he assured her. 'I hope you manage to sleep well after all this excitement.'

'I hope so — but I think my mind might be too active. It's been quite a night, hasn't it?'

'I don't reckon I'll sleep much tonight either, but we both need to. We have lots to do.'

David started to walk away, but then turned back suddenly and grabbed Eve's arms. He gazed deep into her eyes and held her close for several moments before lowering his mouth to hers and kissing her deeply, passionately, searchingly . . . and then he turned and left.

He had so wanted to feel Eve's beautiful lips against his again, but he wasn't ready for any deeper involvement yet and so he felt unable to linger.

Eve, stunned, couldn't move for a moment. She watched David go and waved to him as he got into his car.

Going back inside, she poured herself another gin and tonic; she was trembling again and needed to calm down. She knew she had to start planning the menu for the dinner party, but all she could think about was that last kiss.

She took a large swig of her drink and tried to concentrate on the menu. It couldn't be too complicated as she wasn't the best cook in the world, but every dish had to look as if it had been difficult to make. And, most of all, everything had to taste good.

Before she knew it, it was after midnight and she had dozed off on the sofa.

17

Eve woke up early on the day of her dinner party, but she lay in bed thinking for a while, remembering David's powerful arms around her and his hungry lips on hers. Memories of the past week and all the confusion with Robert and Alison had faded away into obscurity. Since they had left, she had been finding it hard to concentrate on anything else apart from her budding relationship with David, but she knew she had to focus on the party for now.

From the table at the side of her bed Eve picked up a piece of paper on which she had scribbled her menu, and glanced at it. She was still smarting over Betty's treatment of her and she wanted to put her down a peg or two. She intended to show off her cooking, but had she put enough thought and effort into the menu? And then again, did it really matter? The purpose of the evening was to learn more about Phyllis and John, not to get back at Betty.

Eve shivered. What if she was also inviting danger back into her life?

Everyone Eve had asked agreed to come, but Betty's first thought had been to decline, wondering why she was on the guest list. She was always suspicious of Eve's motives. However she knew David would be there, and wondered whether Eve had made a move on him yet. Perhaps he had responded, and Eve wanted to parade their new relationship in public.

Betty knew there was little she could do about that now. She had tried to keep David and Eve apart, but it had been a complete waste of time. The night before she had spoken to Alison on the phone and had been dismayed to hear that her niece had only been interested in talking about Robert. Perhaps if Alison and Robert had still been on Crete, she would have been able to continue manipulating the situation . . . but they were in London, while David and Eve were here.

Betty couldn't think of anyone else who would be suitable for David. Phyllis was the only other single Englishwoman she was friendly with, and it was too soon after Len's death for her to get involved with someone else. In any case, she was too old and dull for David. However, Betty still cherished a faint hope that there might be something she could do to prevent Eve from ensnaring David. She had to keep a close eye on them, and therefore it made sense to go to the dinner party.

Annie was fed up with her social life revolving around The Black Cat, and was looking forward to having dinner at Eve's, but she was surprised to hear that Betty and Don had also been invited. There was certainly no love lost between Betty and Eve, and she didn't expect the evening to pass without an argument.

After all that Eve had been through lately with David and the attempts on her life, Annie was pleased to hear her sounding hopeful and upbeat on the phone. Eve had told her excitedly that she had been out for a drink with David and that they had sorted things out. Perhaps she wanted to show Betty that her meddling had got her nowhere.

Annie knew that Betty wouldn't be too happy, and she wondered whether she had decided to come in the hope of stirring up trouble. Annie thought sadly how foolish and unkind it was to interfere in the lives of others, and she hoped that things had finally settled down for David and Eve.

Knowing that Eve had little time for her, Phyllis was surprised to be invited to dinner, but then, she recalled, she had been helpful after Eve had become sick at her drinks party. As she was always nervous in social situations, Phyllis wasn't sure about attending, but Betty and Don were going so perhaps it wouldn't be too bad. Also, like Annie she didn't go out much apart from occasional visits to The Black Cat.

Eve had decided to have an upmarket barbecue. Even though she was a vegetarian she would cook meat for guests, but she preferred not to and was pleased when David said he would look after the grill. As she had wanted to impress Betty, she had scoured her cookery books to find some exciting recipes for side dishes and salads. In the end, she had decided on a Middle Eastern salad with avocado, raisins and almonds mixed together in an orange flavoured dressing, and a rocket salad with sun dried tomatoes and Parmesan shavings. They weren't difficult to make, but they looked elegant and tasted delicious. She had also decided to prepare a couple of hot dishes, and chose mushrooms in a spicy tomato sauce and baked feta. For dessert, she made tiramisu and a chocolate mousse. Both had also been straight-forward to make, but they looked beautiful. Betty would think she had slaved in the kitchen all day.

David arrived during the afternoon to help Eve get everything set up. He was worried about the evening and couldn't imagine how they could find out anything about Phyllis and John. After all, Eve couldn't just ask her if they had been having an affair! David feared it was going to be a non-event, or worse still a disaster . . . but he had to be there to keep an eye on Eve.

He glanced across at her as she stood folding napkins, and remembered their last kiss. He wished they were going to spend the evening alone, and imagined holding and kissing her again — but that would have to wait until the other guests had left at the end of the evening.

'Have you planned how you're going to approach Phyllis tonight, Eve?' he asked nervously.

'It's difficult,' she replied. 'I think we need to steer the conversation towards John. As there still hasn't been any progress with getting our houses finished, everybody will be keen to talk about him. Then I'll ask Phyllis what she thought of him and we'll need to watch her closely and see how she reacts to his name.'

'Okay — but I'm starting to get a bad feeling about all this, Eve. Could it really have been Phyllis who killed John, poisoned you and tampered with the brakes on your car? If it was, you could be putting yourself in danger again. And then, of course, there's Laura's death and Ken being run over. It just seems too much for one woman to accomplish. Especially someone as timid and nervous as Phyllis.'

'I know — it does seem unbelievable, but I've always thought that once you kill, it gets easier to kill again,' Eve replied. 'Don't worry about me, though. I'll be careful. And after all, I've got you watching over me now!'

David smiled, but inwardly he felt sick with nerves.

'Perhaps it might be better if *I* asked

if she knew John,' David added. 'It might seem less suspicious coming from me.'

Eve nodded in agreement. Not only was it a good idea, but she was delighted to hear how worried David was for her. Even if they didn't find out anything about Phyllis and John, at least Betty would be able to see how well they were getting on.

★　★　★

The rest of the afternoon went quickly and soon it was almost time for the guests to arrive. Eve left David downstairs with a drink while she went and got ready. She didn't have much time, but her dress was hung out waiting and at least she had washed and blow-dried her hair before he had arrived. It only needed a little hairspray.

David was surprised to see Eve come back down so quickly. She looked even more desirable, and again he wished that they could be alone this evening.

Pete and Annie were the first to arrive. Eve complimented her friend on her new hairstyle, thinking how much younger she now looked. Eve had thought from the beginning that Annie was naturally pretty, but could look much better than she did. After all, it didn't take that much effort to go to the hairdressers or to put on make-up, she reasoned.

David went and got drinks for them as Don and Betty arrived; Betty had also had her hair done. Eve smiled to herself; since she had come to Crete, the women all seemed to be making more of an effort with their appearance and she decided that she was a very good influence on them all.

Don and Betty had brought Phyllis along with them. Eve wondered whether Phyllis ever went anywhere on her own, but then she remembered the letter. Phyllis had certainly managed some things without Betty . . . romance certainly, and possibly even murder!

She was certainly a woman to be wary of.

David made sure that everyone had a drink and they all went and sat out on the patio. It was still warm and the sun hadn't quite set, giving a beautiful orange glow to the sky. David started to cook the meat, leaving Eve to entertain the guests. She thought it best to keep the conversation light until they started eating, knowing it would be better if David were there to help steer the conversation in the right direction. She knew she was prone to rushing into things, and didn't want to ask too many questions too early on.

Besides, it might be best if Phyllis had a few drinks first to make her less inhibited. She had asked for a gin and tonic, and Eve whispered to David to pour her a large measure.

About fifteen minutes later, Eve went over to David to see how the meat was coming on. She deliberately put her arm around him, and was sure she could feel Betty's eyes on the back of her head. Smiling, she kissed David on the cheek and rejoined the others.

Betty ignored her and Annie grinned, thinking that this must have been the point of the dinner party after all. Eve obviously wanted to show Betty that all her plans to keep David from her hadn't worked, and although she felt that Eve was being a little childish, Betty did deserve it.

'The meat's almost done,' David called out.

'Great,' Eve replied. 'I'll top up your drinks and go and get the rest of the food.'

Eve handed Phyllis another large gin and tonic before going into the kitchen.

Annie thought Eve had prepared too much food, imagining that she was trying to make Betty feel small. Still, it all looked good and she was looking forward to sampling everything.

Looking at the food, both David and Annie thought Eve had surpassed herself, but Betty looked grim and was even more miserable when the hot mushrooms and baked feta came out. Then David presented the meat. Betty was astounded to see that there was chicken, lamb and steak, plus veggie burgers and veggie sausages for Eve. The first thought that went through her mind was that Eve was showing off again, trying to make her feel inferior. She looked at the array of food, thinking that there was enough to feed an army. Why had she decided to come?

'Come on everybody, dig in!' Eve said.

'This all looks wonderful,' Phyllis remarked. 'I haven't had such a feast in ages.'

'Well, I hope you all enjoy it. Just help yourself to more drink as well when you want it. There's plenty.'

They started to eat and even Betty filled her plate, reluctantly admitting it was delicious. However, nothing had yet been said about John. Eve was getting impatient and wondered whether she should bring up the subject, but then David spoke.

'Has there been any more news about the outstanding work on your properties?'

'Nothing,' Betty replied. 'This is getting absolutely ridiculous. Before we know it, it'll be winter and it'll start raining. Then a lot of the work will have to wait until next year.'

'I went into John's office yesterday,' Pete said. 'But I was just brushed off. Mind you, I think that the woman in there doesn't know much.'

'She's in there every day, so she must be getting paid,' Betty exclaimed. 'There has to be some money somewhere.'

'Who knows?' Pete continued. 'There's more bad news as well, I'm afraid. I bumped into Petros yesterday, and he said the police have put the murder to the back of their books. They don't seem to think they're going to be able to solve it, so they aren't doing much. There have been a couple more robberies lately, so they're concentrating on them. I don't know if you've heard,' he went on, 'but one was at gunpoint. The couple were just sitting at home when two men broke in and threatened them.'

'Oh no,' Eve gasped. 'That's awful! I suppose we'll have to blame the economic crisis, won't we? What with all these extra taxes and everything going up, it's making people desperate. Still, that poor couple sat at home! Who were they? Does anyone know them?'

'It was the Parkers,' Pete carried on. 'They've been here for a couple of months, though we haven't met them. They keep themselves to themselves from what I've heard. I believe they weren't hurt, but the robbers got away with some jewellery and a laptop. I think the Parkers have decided to go back to England, but I don't know how easy it will be for them to sell the house.'

'It must have been a terrible ordeal,' Eve said, shivering.

Everybody went quiet and after a few minutes, Eve thought it was about time she brought Phyllis into the conversation. She hadn't yet discovered anything about her relationship with John.

'I know John Phillips is dead, but he certainly has a lot to answer for. I don't know anyone who has a nice word to say about him. What about you, Phyllis? Did you know John? I know you didn't have your house built by him, but did you ever meet?'

'No! I didn't know him. I didn't know him at all,' Phyllis answered quickly and sharply. 'Why would you ask that?'

Everybody was dumbfounded, and even Betty was surprised by Phyllis's outburst. By acting as if she were guilty of something, Phyllis had surprised them all, and David got the impression that nobody knew about the affair — not even Betty.

But they were certainly all curious now to know why she had acted so defensively.

'I'm sorry, Phyllis, I didn't mean to upset you,' Eve continued quickly. 'I wasn't suggesting you had any kind of relationship with John. I was only wondering what impression you had of him. He had issues with so many people, I just wondered if you felt the same.'

Phyllis however, didn't calm down, and Eve thought anxiously that she might have given her a little too much gin.

'Next you'll be saying it was me who killed him! Oh, and Laura as well, not to mention that it was probably me who tried to kill you and Ken. Why not blame Phyllis — it's always the quiet one, isn't it?' Phyllis blurted out. 'I had nothing to do with John, nothing at all. I really don't know why you're making all these accusations, Eve.'

'Calm down!' Betty admonished. 'Nobody thinks you murdered him. Eve is just being her usual bumbling self. Take no notice of her.'

Eve looked angrily at Betty. How dare she?

'I'm sorry,' Phyllis said, beginning to quieten down. 'I don't know what came over me. The police questioning everyone has made me nervous. I don't know why I'm on edge. It's just the way I am, I suppose. You hear all these awful things about the wrong person being arrested, and being in a foreign country as well is pretty scary. But no, Eve, I didn't know John at all. I saw him in The Black Cat now and again, but that was it. I never talked to him, nor did I want to.'

'I'm sorry, Phyllis,' Eve said, trying to sound apologetic.

Things had got a bit out of hand and Eve was relieved that Phyllis had started to talk a little more sanely. Eve didn't want her to become suspicious — but was it too late?

'I don't blame you for not wanting to know John,' Eve continued. 'I only met him when I came over in February to choose my house, but I thought there was something not quite right about him.'

'But you still bought from him,' Betty observed.

'And so did you,' Eve replied quickly.

The two women stared stonily at each other.

'Annie, what's wrong?' said David suddenly, interrupting the cold silence between the two women.

Everyone turned and saw Annie wiping away a few tears.

'Oh, I'm so sorry. Hearing Laura's name reminded me of her. It seems such a waste of a young life.'

Silence fell once more over the group of neighbours.

'Phyllis,' Eve ventured. 'I remember seeing you talking to Laura outside the shop in the village the day before she was found murdered. Was she okay? Did she say anything that might give us a clue as to who might have murdered her?'

By this time, Phyllis seemed completely calm and didn't flinch as she spoke. 'She said that she was scared Yiannis was going to kill her. I've already told the police this.'

Eve looked at Phyllis. Was she telling the truth? Eve had thought the two women had been engaged in a heated conversation, and if Laura had said she was frightened, Phyllis would have been comforting her, not arguing.

'Come on, everybody,' Don said, breaking the silence. 'This is getting silly. We've been invited for a lovely dinner, so let's talk about more cheerful things. There's not much we can do about John's murder or about getting our homes completed. We've put our complaints about our properties in so many times without success and I can't think of anything else we can do.'

'You're right, Don,' Eve said. 'Let's just enjoy the meal. I've made two desserts, so do leave room to try both of them!'

The rest of the evening went by without any mention of John. After having a few drinks, Betty relaxed and even started to flirt with David. Eve smiled; and at least Betty wasn't having a go at her any more.

Don and Pete talked about football and Eve and Annie about David. Annie was pleased that he and Eve were getting closer. Although Eve could be a difficult woman, she had a good heart and Annie imagined a stronger woman like Eve would suit David. While it would be better if he were a little more forceful and decisive, perhaps what Eve needed was a gentle and kind man to quieten her down.

Phyllis sat next to Annie and Eve, but despite their attempts to bring her into the conversation, it was futile. After her emotional display she was reluctant to say anything else, and was just interested in drinking wine.

Annie was worried about Phyllis. She was acting completely out of character this evening. Nobody had ever heard her speak as she had earlier, nor had they seen her drink so much, but nobody chastised her, not even Betty. All were a little apprehensive that she might flare up again.

It was one o'clock when the dinner party ended. The only person still there half an hour later, was David. He had stayed to help Eve tidy up, hoping that they might be able to relax together for a while.

'Well, I don't think we got much out of that, did we?' he asked later. 'But it was a wonderful meal, despite Phyllis's display. And it was very entertaining once Betty got a little drunk. I hope you didn't mind that I let her flirt with me?'

'Of course not,' Eve said, happy that he was concerned for her feelings. 'But you're wrong,' she continued. 'We got plenty from the evening. From the way Phyllis reacted, it's obvious she was having an affair with John.'

'Well, I don't think we had much doubt of that. The letter spoke for itself.'

'I thought about that,' Eve replied. 'It could have been written by someone else and planted there, but after this evening, I definitely think Phyllis was in love with John.'

'But what do we do now?' David asked, a little wary of how Eve would reply. 'We have no proof that she killed him, nor did she have a motive.'

'John could have ended their relationship. That would be motive enough. I think the only thing for me to do is to go and talk to her about him. She probably knows I suspect she had an affair with him, and probably wants to know how I found out.'

'You need to be careful, Eve,' David said, a worried look coming over his face. 'If she did kill John, she's probably the one who tried to kill you, and I have an awful feeling she wouldn't hesitate to try again. And what about Laura — and Ken?'

'They must have found out something about Phyllis killing John. Though I am surprised about my car. She doesn't even drive, so how would she know how to tamper with my brakes?'

'I have no idea. I'm not much good

with cars either, apart from driving them!'

Eve thought for a moment and David knew she was planning her next move. He dreaded knowing what it was.

'I'll go and talk to Phyllis tomorrow,' Eve finally announced. 'I don't want to leave it long enough for her to think of another way to get rid of me.'

'I'll go with you. It'll be safer.'

'No — I don't think she'll talk at all with you there. I promise I'll tread carefully and won't accuse her of murder. I'll make it clear that I don't think she was the one who murdered John, and suggest helping her try and find who killed the man she loved. I'll pretend to be her friend.'

'I don't like it, Eve. I really don't.'

David thought he couldn't bear to lose Eve now and he moved towards her. He stroked her cheek, and although she smiled, she seemed preoccupied.

Unable to forget their time in John's house, he desperately wanted to kiss her again. He also thought that if he did, it might take her mind off the murder. If she thought there was a future with him, she might not be so reckless and wouldn't confront Phyllis on her own.

He reached down and as their lips met. Eve melted into his arms and she forgot all about Phyllis. As David became more passionate, Eve thought this could be the night for them to be together. Finally, she gently took his hand and started to lead him upstairs — but then there was a knock at the door.

'Who on earth is that?' Eve exclaimed. 'What if it's Phyllis coming back to do something to me?'

'I doubt she'll do anything with me around,' David said.

Eve looked at David gratefully. She felt safe with him and was relieved when he went to answer the door.

'I'm so sorry to bother you, David.' Eve heard Betty's loud voice. 'Unfortunately our car won't start. I have no idea what's wrong with it and Don

is useless with anything mechanical.
Could you help us?'

Eve appeared at the door. Betty
looked smug and she wondered if the
woman would ever stop interfering.

'Apart from changing tyres, I'm
afraid I'm not much good with cars
either,' David said. 'But I suppose I
could give you all a lift home. Then you
can get someone to look at it
tomorrow.'

'Oh, that would be lovely,' Betty
answered, smiling broadly.

'You'll be okay, won't you, Eve?'
David asked.

'I'll be fine,' Eve replied, even though
she was disappointed.

He didn't want to leave her, but
when she had started to lead him
towards the stairs, he had become a
little apprehensive. He wanted her so
much, but it had been a long time
since he'd been intimate with a
woman. His marriage had been a
failure and he didn't want to go
through anything like that again. He

hoped he could get his head straight before Eve got fed up of him pulling away from her.

As he said goodnight David thought how desirable Eve was. There was an air of vulnerability around her this evening, and he felt lucky that she had chosen him. He gave her a gentle kiss before he left, and he shivered when she touched him and murmured goodnight. He was pleased he'd kissed her in front of Betty; he didn't like people meddling in his life.

As Eve shut the door, she felt herself glowing inside. David had kissed her in front of Betty, and although it wasn't the overwhelmingly passionate kiss they had shared earlier, that didn't matter. It was still a kiss.

Eve felt sure Betty had done something to the car so that she could get David away from her, but did it matter? Betty could do what she wanted, because Eve had no doubts about her relationship with David any more.

She made herself focus on Phyllis. She had to be her priority for the time being, and the sooner she proved Phyllis was the murderer, the sooner she could be with David.

18

Eve woke with a throbbing headache. She hadn't drunk much the previous evening and wondered why she was feeling fragile. Apart from one small gin and tonic, she'd just had a couple of glasses of wine, so perhaps the stress of holding a dinner party had taken its toll. Although she always enjoyed playing the hostess, yesterday had been hard work and a long day — not forgetting the excitement of Phyllis's outburst.

Looking at the clock, Eve was surprised to see it was already half past ten, but then it had been after three when she had finally got into bed. She had sat up for a long time, thinking of the best way to approach Phyllis. After last night's performance. Eve believed her to be unpredictable and potentially dangerous. Phyllis had acted completely out of character, and in trying to convince everybody that she hadn't known John, she had given the opposite impression. Even Betty had been surprised.

Eve stretched, but she didn't want to get up yet. She was comfortable and felt her bed was the best place to think everything through. She was certain that Phyllis and John had been lovers, but if she had cared for him as much as her letter had suggested, why would she kill him? Perhaps they had split up and she had gone to his house to confront him about their break-up. Things might have gone badly and she could have hit him on the head in the heat of the moment.

Eve wondered if she was taking on more than she could handle, knowing that if Phyllis had murdered John, there was little doubt that she had poisoned her and tampered with her car, killed Laura for whatever reason, and later tried to kill Ken. And on top of everything, after last night Phyllis probably thought Eve knew too much and might go to any lengths to silence her.

Finally, Eve got up, showered and dressed and started putting on her make-up. She didn't look her best this morning and thought she could see bags under her eyes, but started to feel more like herself again as she painted and powdered her face.

Having completed her morning ritual, Eve went downstairs to get some headache tablets, and then realised she was hungry. It was already well after eleven so she finished off the salad from the previous night, with a couple of slices of bread and olive oil. A little tiramisu was left as well. She thought that perhaps she was turning out to be a good cook after all. Knowing she had overdone the amounts, she was pleased that there wasn't a lot of food left over from the party. Everybody had tucked in and complimented her on her efforts — even Betty.

* * *

After enjoying her brunch, Eve called Portia, having decided that her dog should come with her to see Phyllis. Although Portia was a gentle dog, she looked fierce and was protective of her mistress. Eve was certain she would guard her if she were threatened, but as she arrived at Phyllis's home, she began to doubt her decision. What if Phyllis hurt Portia? However, she tried to put these thoughts out of her head, telling herself that her imagination was working overtime again.

Eve hesitated for a moment and then knocked. When nobody answered, she knocked again, but there was still no reply.

Was Phyllis out, or was she was hiding? Eve walked around the house, but it was quiet. She had wanted to confront her today and now she felt deflated.

Even so, she still wasn't certain of the best way to approach her. Perhaps she should first apologise for upsetting her last night and then gauge her reaction, but if Phyllis accepted her apology, she would be no further forward. Maybe she should just ask her outright if she had been having an affair with John, but if Phyllis reacted as she had last night, it could be dangerous. At least with her not being in, Eve had more time to think about her next move.

She headed for home, taking a longer route so as to give Portia a good walk. It was hot, but they kept in the shade of the olive trees. Apart from the trees, everything looked dry, and Eve was looking forward to seeing the spring flowers again. Poppies appeared as early as February, and she remembered seeing the almond trees covered in blossom.

After about an hour, Eve went home to give Portia food and water and left her there while she headed back to Phyllis's.

The woman still hadn't returned and Eve wondered where she could be.

Phyllis had said she spent most of her time at home.

As Eve started to think about giving up, Don drove by and stopped when he saw her.

'Hi there! Wonderful evening last night. Thanks again for inviting us. The food was fantastic. Fit for a king!'

'I'm glad you enjoyed it,' Eve replied, glowing with pleasure.

Don was about to drive off when Eve shouted out, 'Don, wait a minute! I wanted a word with Phyllis. Have you seen her?'

'She's gone shopping in Rethymnon with Betty. They've taken the bus and won't be back until later in the day. Can I give her a message? She's coming back to our house for supper.'

'No, it wasn't anything important. Thanks anyway.'

Eve wandered back home. Having got psyched up for her meeting with Phyllis, it now had to wait, and she didn't know what to do for the rest of the day. Still, she was glad to get home.

It was hot and her feet hurt after so much walking. Collapsing on the sofa, Eve decided she would leave trying to see Phyllis until tomorrow. If she was eating with Don and Betty tonight, Phyllis wouldn't get home until late and Eve wasn't keen on walking to her house in the dark.

It was now mid-afternoon and Eve decided to put on her bikini. Taking a book with her, she went outside, but after about half an hour she drifted into a deep, dreamless sleep.

★ ★ ★

A little later, Eve's mobile woke her. She leapt off her sun bed, not wanting to miss the call in case it was Phyllis. Don might have told her that she was looking for her — but if so, what was she going to say? She still hadn't devised a proper plan.

'Good evening.' A familiar voice spoke.

Hearing it was David, Eve felt safe

and secure again. 'Hi there! I thought you were meeting your friend, Tony in Chania?'

'I'm going out soon. I just wanted to know how you got on with Phyllis today.'

David sounded almost relieved when he heard about Eve's wasted journeys. 'I can't say I'm sorry,' he said. 'I've been on edge today worrying about you.'

'Don't be. I'll be careful. There's nothing I can do until tomorrow now, anyway.'

'If you change your mind and want me to go with you, give me a ring. Though I'd rather you didn't go at all.'

'Thank you, but it's something I have to do and it's better if I do it on my own. Look, you go off and have a good time tonight. I'll phone you tomorrow.'

Eve smiled as she put down the receiver. It felt good to have somebody care for her this much.

David, however, was worried about Eve. There could only be so many times that she would be able to cheat death.

A little later, after Eve had showered and got dressed, she dozed on the sofa with BB King playing in the background. She knew she was being lazy, but the previous day had been extremely hectic and she didn't feel guilty.

She was imagining spending a romantic evening at home with David. There would be candlelight, champagne and music and he would take her in his arms and kiss her, first slowly, and then with increasing desire. Then they would go up to her bedroom and he would slowly undress her and . . .

Suddenly, Eve was brought back down to earth by a knock on the door. She sat up quickly. She wasn't expecting anyone. David certainly wouldn't be back from Chania yet. When the knocking started again, Portia barked and Eve was relieved that her dog was with her. At least whoever it was might think twice about hurting her. She got up and quietly crept towards the door, wondering, why she was pretending to be out. Her car was parked outside, the lights were on, and whoever it was could hear the music.

'Who's there?' Eve called, knowing there was no point sounding scared.

'It's only me, Phyllis. Don said you were looking for me earlier today, so I thought I'd pop in and see what you wanted.'

Eve felt her stomach churn. What excuse could she give for going to Phyllis's house earlier in the day? And why hadn't she decided what she was going to say to her, instead of daydreaming about David? Then Eve wondered why Phyllis had bothered to come over this late. It could easily have waited until morning. After all, she had told Don it wasn't important — and Eve's house wasn't even on Phyllis's route home. She knew she had no choice but to open the door. She needed to think quickly.

'Sorry to have taken so long,' Eve

said, trying to smile. 'I was dozing on the sofa and I wasn't quite awake when you knocked. Come in.'

Eve guided Phyllis into the sitting room. 'Please, sit down. Would you like a drink?' Eve felt that she definitely needed one.

'A gin and tonic would be lovely,' Phyllis replied.

Eve thought Phyllis had started drinking too much — but then perhaps so had she, since the first attempt on her life. Attempting to hide her mounting fear she said, 'I think I'll join you,' as she went to get the drinks and opened a couple of packets of crisps. She hadn't had any supper yet; she didn't want to get tipsy and lose control of the situation.

They both sat down, and for once Eve didn't know what to say. However, Phyllis pre-empted her.

'Was there anything special you wanted?' Phyllis asked. 'I was surprised you had come to see me.'

Eve knew she had to get things

together before Phyllis became even more suspicious.

'I just wanted to apologise for upsetting you last night. I didn't mean anything by it.'

Phyllis stared and Eve noticed there was a strange look in her eyes. She was calm and in control, nothing like the Phyllis everyone knew. Phyllis took a large gulp of her drink.

'You know, don't you?' she asked coldly. 'You know that John and I had an affair.'

'An affair? I had no idea!' Eve lied, hoping she sounded convincing. 'How on earth would I have found out?'

'I don't know, but you did. You're always snooping around.'

Eve was now becoming truly afraid of Phyllis.

'Who would have told me?' Eve asked, trying not to sound scared. 'Betty would never confide in me. She hates me.'

'Betty doesn't know. Nobody does. John and I were discreet.'

'I don't understand,' Eve stuttered. 'Everybody says how much you loved your husband. How could you have had an affair with someone else so soon after he died?'

'You know nothing about me,' Phyllis said harshly. 'I'm the sort of woman people like you dismiss. You think I lack strength of character and you've had no interest in getting to know me.'

Phyllis was right and Eve felt a pang of guilt. She was rarely curious about people who were dull and quiet.

'Well, let me tell you a bit about myself,' Phyllis continued, barely pausing for breath.

Eve thought that after years of keeping everything in, Phyllis was going to pour her heart out. She was apprehensive of where it might lead and wished that David were there to protect her.

'At the age of eighteen,' Phyllis went on, 'I went straight from living with my parents to being a wife. I've never had to be on my own. There was always somebody to look after me. Then my husband died and I was left alone in a foreign country. Betty took me under her wing, but she smothered me. There's a difference between someone looking after you and someone taking over your life. She always bosses me around and never listens to a word I say. You've seen what she's like.

'I hated it, but she helped with all the legal stuff after my husband died. I couldn't have done it on my own. Then one day, three months after Len died, I went for a long walk and ended up in a bar miles away from here.'

Eve wondered what Len had been like, but didn't get a chance to ask.

'I sat there drinking wine and crying,' Phyllis went on. 'Everything was so awful. I didn't have enough money to go back to England, and what would I have done there, anyway? My parents are dead and I don't have children. England might be a familiar country, but I would still have been alone.'

Eve started to feel a little sorry for

her, realising how lucky she had been in the way her life had turned out.

'Then after I'd drunk half a litre of wine, John walked by,' Phyllis continued. 'He could see I'd been crying and asked if I was okay. I burst into tears again and he gave me a tissue and sat down. Then he ordered more wine and we chatted for hours. I couldn't believe how kind he was and how interested he was in my story. Everybody was always saying how ruthless and hard he was, but he wasn't.'

'So that's when it started — your affair with John?'

'Yes, he seemed genuine. He was the first man I had made love to since my husband died. In fact, he was only the second man I had ever been with. I got married so young, you see.'

Eve found it hard to believe that a woman in her fifties had only slept with two men, but it was romantic that Phyllis had been faithful to her husband. Too few people were these days.

Eve's thoughts drifted momentarily, imagining what it would be like to be David's wife. She would definitely be faithful to him, and she thought how amazing their life could be . . . but would it be too claustrophobic? She needed space to do her own thing, but she was pretty certain that David wouldn't want to be with her twenty-four hours a day.

Eve had almost stopped listening to Phyllis; she liked to be the centre of attention and could get bored if people just talked about themselves. But she knew she had to concentrate on her visitor and stop thinking about David.

When she looked at Phyllis, she realised she was crying. 'There, there,' Eve said. 'It's okay.'

'No. No, it's not. I loved him so much. I miss him. Why did he end our relationship like that? He'd still be here if he hadn't.'

Eve gasped and Phyllis realised she'd said too much.

'You did kill him, didn't you?' Eve cried. 'He dumped you and you killed him!'

'What? I couldn't have killed him — I loved him! Are you accusing me of murder?'

Eve wished she hadn't said anything. Why didn't she think before speaking, and why wasn't David here? She felt vulnerable and scared.

'I'm sorry,' Eve said quickly. 'I don't know what made me say that. Of course you didn't kill him. I think I've had a little too much to drink and I'm talking a lot of rubbish.'

'We've probably both said more than we intended,' Phyllis replied coldly. 'Perhaps we could have a coffee? It might clear our heads a bit.'

Eve got up, hoping that Phyllis would dismiss what she had said, and went into the kitchen.

A few minutes later, she came back in with the coffee. She had wanted to phone David, but she still didn't have a landline and her mobile was on the table by the sofa. Phyllis would have seen her pick it up.

Eve was now convinced that Phyllis had not only killed John, but had also tried to kill her, and she was terrified. Trying to smile, she knew she had to be calm — but as she put the tray down, Phyllis pulled out a gun.

Eve stared, unable to move or say anything. Why hadn't she listened to David and Annie and kept her nose out of everything?

'Phyllis . . . ' Eve stammered. 'Put the gun down . . . please. What do you hope to gain? David knows about you and John, and everyone's suspicious after last night. You'll be the prime suspect if you kill me. You'd never get off this island before they arrested you.'

'Don't you think I've thought this through? You all think I'm weak and stupid, but I'm not. If I kill you this evening, you won't be found until tomorrow. I have a ticket on the last flight out of Chania tonight. Once I'm on the mainland, I'll be long gone before the police even start searching for me.'

'The police will put two and two together and you'll be arrested when you get off the plane in London.'

'I don't think so. They'll question people here and then search the island first. Come on — you know they won't be that quick. And anyway, who says I'm going to London?'

Eve felt herself about to cry. She glanced around the room. Phyllis was calm and appeared capable of pulling the trigger.

'If you're looking for your dog, I let her out,' Phyllis said.

Eve didn't know what to do. Portia wasn't there to protect her now — but at least the dog was safe. Eve knew she had to find some way of stalling Phyllis.

'If you are going to kill me, please at least do me the decency of telling me what happened between you and John. I wouldn't want to go to my grave without ever knowing the truth.'

'You want to know my story?' Phyllis

asked, laughing. 'I know you're trying to delay the inevitable or put me off guard. It won't work, but if you're really that interested, I'll tell you. I'm in no rush. I have plenty of time to catch my plane . . .

'Well, John and I were getting on really well, or so I thought. It was fun sneaking around. Everybody seemed so sorry for me, but I was having the time of my life — the sex was great, much better than with Len.'

Phyllis paused, relishing the astonished look in Eve's eyes. Eve couldn't believe how different Phyllis was to what they had thought her to be. It was completely unnerving.

'John took me out to dinner in Rethymnon so that we wouldn't be seen together,' Phyllis continued. 'He wined and dined me and bought me presents. Everyone thought he was mean, but he wasn't.

'Then things changed when I suggested we tell other people about us. I had wanted to keep it secret in the beginning because it was so soon after Len's death, but as time went on, I wanted to show off that we were a couple. John wouldn't have any of it. I kept asking him why, but then one day I saw him in The Black Cat with a beautiful young woman . . . he seemed so animated and alive.

'Naturally, I was jealous and confronted him about it. He said she was just a client and he kissed me and took me to bed. I thought everything was okay between us, but then a letter came from him ending our relationship. I couldn't believe it. Although he said he just needed some space, I felt there must have been something going on between him and that other woman. He said he felt our relationship was getting too serious and he wasn't at a place in his life where he wanted to settle down. He was in his early fifties and had never been married! When *would* he be ready for a commitment?'

Eve was relieved that Phyllis was talking so much and hoped that it might take her mind off killing her, but the gun was still pointed in her direction.

Eve couldn't think of anything else to do. Perhaps David would pop in after his evening in Chania and rescue her, but he'd probably be too late. She knew she had to keep Phyllis talking for as long as possible.

'That's terrible,' Eve said angrily. 'How dare he treat you like that? What a coward — ending your affair with a letter.'

Phyllis thought it was a pity Eve knew so much. They were on the same wavelength and they could have been friends if things had been different. Eve was bossy, but she was much more fun than Betty. The fact that she was attractive and men flocked around her could mean that one of them might have taken a fancy to her instead. Still, there was no point thinking about that, now that it was too late.

'You're right. It was terrible the way John ended our relationship,' Phyllis continued. 'I was hurt and angry and I wasn't going to leave everything like it was. I wanted to tell him face to face that he was weak, so I went over to his house.

'But when I got there, all I could do was beg him to take me back. I kept asking him why he was doing this and I made a complete fool of myself.

'He said he didn't want to talk about us any more and that we were finished. He refused to give me any more reasons why he didn't want me, and he just laughed. I knew then that everyone had been right about him. He was ruthless and cold. He seemed so smug sitting there with his whisky and cigar, so I calmly picked up his ornament of Aphrodite and hit him on the head. How ironic — Aphrodite, the goddess of love, killed him!

'I didn't mean to do it, but when I realised he was dead, a peculiar feeling of relief overwhelmed me. It was what he deserved for treating me as he had. But I decided there and then that I wasn't going to jail.

'So I went into the kitchen and found a pair of rubber gloves. First I wiped my fingerprints off everything I thought I'd touched and then I ransacked the house. I stole his money and gun to make it look like a burglary and took the ornament with me, throwing it into the sea. I'm not as stupid as people think.'

'No, you're a very clever woman, Phyllis,' Eve agreed in admiration. 'I take it that it was you who tried to kill me as well?'

'You were snooping around far too much. I didn't plan to actually kill you with the arsenic, just make you sick. If you were ill, you wouldn't have the energy to keep snooping around.'

'But what about Laura?'

'Laura? Stupid girl — she was blackmailing me!'

'What — Laura? Blackmailing you? I don't believe it!'

'Yes, but she didn't know who she was dealing with. You were right, you know, when you said you thought you saw her coming out of my house the day you were driving back from Hari's. She had come to tell me she had seen me with John in Rethymnon a while back having dinner, saw us holding hands and kissing and said she'd tell the police if I didn't give her money.'

'I can't believe that,' Eve said, genuinely surprised. 'She was such a lovely girl — or so I thought.'

'Actually, you're not that wrong about her. She only wanted the money to get out of the country and away from Yiannis. Apparently he took all her wages, so she was stuck here on Crete with a man who physically abused her.'

'Is that what you were arguing about outside the shop the day before she was killed?'

'She needed more money than she originally asked for and I said I didn't have it. I finally agreed to give it to her that night, but in the end I decided she had to die. Even if she left the country, she still would have known about me and John and I would never have felt safe. I arranged to meet her with the cash, but instead, I killed her. That's when John's gun came in useful.'

'What about my car? How did you know how to do that? You can't even drive.'

'Well . . . actually I can.'

Eve gasped. Phyllis was a woman of many secrets.

'More than that — for a few years my husband had his own small garage and I learned a lot about cars. Not that it's difficult to cut the hydraulic brake lines on a car.

'I'm sure you're going to ask about Ken next so I'll save you the time. The day before he was run over, I was sitting at the bar in The Black Cat having a G and T, and I started chatting to a couple of tourists. I think killing people has made me so much more outgoing, don't you? Anyway, we were talking about jobs and such-like and I mentioned helping out in Len's garage and how much I enjoyed it and loved driving as well.

'At that moment, Ken dropped a glass. I looked at him and he looked away quickly. I was certain it crossed his mind that if I had been lying about my driving skills, I could be lying about so much more, so he had to be silenced as well. I knew he went to the cash and carry at the same time every Monday night in Chania, so I hired a car and followed him. The rest you know.'

'I was just wondering why you didn't drive here when you first came over?' Eve asked, thinking it strange and — more importantly — trying to keep the conversation going.

'I'm afraid I got too many points on my licence back in England and lost it. I was too embarrassed to tell anyone and pretended I couldn't drive. I have it back now, of course.'

Eve felt time was running out and she didn't know what to do next. Perhaps she should beg Phyllis for mercy and promise to keep her secrets, but she didn't think it would do any good.

'Get up. Get up now,' Phyllis ordered suddenly, pointing the gun straight at Eve's head.

Eve had no choice but to do as she was told. She stood up. Her legs felt like jelly and she didn't know whether or not they would hold her up. Phyllis shoved her and told her to walk towards the basement.

'Go down there,' she shouted, pushing Eve.

Stumbling, Eve felt tears starting to fall. Why on earth had she interfered in the murder enquiries? If she ever got out of this mess, she would never meddle again. She wondered what Phyllis intended to do. Eve had been certain she was going to shoot her, but she hadn't yet. However, she knew too much and she couldn't believe Phyllis would let her live.

'Get a move on,' Phyllis ordered as she followed Eve downstairs, all the while still pointing the gun at her.

The light wasn't working and as Eve tried to find the next step, Phyllis suddenly hit her on the head with the gun. Eve fell down the last couple of stairs and lay motionless on the floor.

Phyllis went and felt her pulse, but even though Eve was still breathing, she didn't finish her off, but quickly ran back upstairs and slammed the basement door shut, locking it behind her. As she entered the sitting room, she heard Portia barking outside.

'Damn that dog,' Phyllis muttered crossly. 'She'll have to be got rid of. Her barking could bring the neighbours over.'

Thinking it might be difficult to shoot an excitable dog, Phyllis went into the kitchen and looked under the sink. There was a tin of rat poison. *Not much in there*, she thought, shaking the container, *but I don't think it'll take a lot to kill her.*

Phyllis found some dog food and mixed in the rat poison. Portia wagged her tail happily when Phyllis went outside to feed her, then the dog's nose went straight into the bowl. Meanwhile Phyllis went into the sitting room with a can of lighter fluid . . .

19

While Eve was having what was turning out to be the worst day of her life, David was in a bar in Chania harbour with his friend, Tony. Tony lived in a village on the opposite side of town from David and Eve, but like them, his property had fantastic views of both the sea and of the White Mountains, and during the summer he loved sitting on his balcony with a beer, immersing himself in his surroundings.

Both men enjoyed walking and had met a couple of summers previously when they had trekked through the spectacular eighteen-kilometre Samaria Gorge.

A couple of friends from England were staying with Tony, and he had arranged for them all to meet David in Chania for a drink. However, Tony could see that David's mind was elsewhere.

David had told him about the murders and a little of what had been happening with Eve, and Tony knew he was worried about her. He'd been amazed to see that David had been so captivated by a woman, knowing that after his failed marriage, he was unwilling to start a serious relationship.

Tony had introduced him to a few women, but all his attempts had ended in failure and he had just about given up trying. Perhaps Eve was the one for him, and for David's sake he hoped she wasn't in danger.

'I can see you can't stop thinking about Eve,' Tony remarked. 'Perhaps you should get back and see if everything's okay?'

'I'm sure she's fine,' David lied rather unconvincingly. 'I'm sorry. I'm ruining your evening.'

'Don't be silly,' Tony replied, grinning. 'My friends are having a whale of a time. Look at them chatting up those girls!'

At that moment, David's mobile rang

and he answered it straight away, hoping it was Eve. He desperately needed to be reassured that she was safe.

'No, Annie,' he replied. 'Eve's not here.'

His face fell as he listened to Annie.

'What is it?' Tony asked, concerned.

'I'm sorry, I'll have to go. Ken's woken up from his coma and remembers Phyllis telling people she could mend cars. I'll phone you tomorrow.'

Tony stared at David. He wasn't certain what that meant, but he was sure Eve was in some sort of trouble.

David found himself almost running to his car. He remembered the way Phyllis had acted at Eve's dinner party, and the more he thought about it, the more he believed that she was the killer — and if he was right, Phyllis wasn't stable and Eve could be in serious danger.

There was so much traffic in town that David thought he'd never get out of Chania, but once he was on the highway, he put his foot down. He knew he was going over the speed limit, but for once he didn't care. A few years previously, speed cameras had been put up along the length of the highway, but they had never been switched on. Also, the police usually weren't around at this time of night, so he didn't think he would be stopped. David hated breaking the law, but he had no choice. He had to make sure Eve was safe.

* * *

Having left Chania hospital a little before David had left the centre of town, Pete and Annie arrived at Eve's place first and were shocked to see flames coming from her sitting room. Not getting a reply at the front door, they rushed round to the back of the house. They found a very sick dog lying on the grass.

'Oh no! What's happened to Portia?' Annie gasped.

'It looks like Phyllis could have

poisoned her,' Pete replied. 'No time to waste. You've got our vet's emergency number, haven't you? Give him a ring and get Portia there as quickly as possible, while I phone the fire brigade and the police.'

Within minutes Annie had dashed back to Chania with Portia, while Pete, finding the back door unlocked, had started trying to to douse the flames. He had no idea where Eve was.

Finally, David reached the village, relieved that he would soon be at Eve's house. He imagined taking her in his arms and kissing her, hoping this was the night they would finally be together. As he approached, he thought he could see flames coming from her house. He stopped the car and rushed to the front door and hammered on it, but nobody answered, so he went to the back where he found the kitchen door open.

'Hey! Is anyone there?' he called out.

'I'm in here!' Pete called back, coughing.

David ran into the sitting room and

saw Pete frantically trying to put out the fire. 'Where's Eve?' he shouted.

'I don't know. Hopefully out,' Pete panted.

David went upstairs, but was unable to find Eve. When he came back down, the fire brigade had turned up and Pete was sitting at the bottom of the stairs, exhausted. He told David what Ken had said about Phyllis and how they had all become concerned for Eve. After not being able to get in touch with her, he and Annie had returned to the village, but had not been able to find her.

'The basement!' David gasped suddenly. He rushed to the basement door and, with help from Pete and one of the firemen, managed to break it down. There was Eve lying sprawled on the floor, just beginning to come round.

'Oh, David, you've come to save me . . . ' she said groggily. 'I knew you would. Oh, dear, my head does hurt . . . '

David helped her sit up, thinking how

vulnerable she really was, and finally admitted he was in love with her. Why had he wasted so much time? He took her in his arms and held her close.

'I'm so relieved you're okay, Eve! I started panicking when I was in Chania, and then Annie phoned to say Ken had woken up. He said he'd overheard Phyllis admit she knew about cars. I had an awful feeling she was going to hurt you.'

Eve held onto David even tighter. She felt his hand stroke her hair, and then he pressed his lips to hers. Despite the pain she was in, Eve felt as if she were flying — underneath that quiet exterior, she realised, was a passionate man. After all they had been through, she finally believed David wanted to be with her.

She was shaking and thought she could hear her heart beating — though whether because of her latest escape from death or because the man she had been dreaming about for so long was finally hers, she wasn't sure.

'Hey,' Pete shouted down. 'Are you okay, Eve?'

Carefully David helped her back upstairs.

'Oh, Pete, it was awful,' Eve murmured, still holding onto David. 'Phyllis tried to kill me! She came here with a gun and admitted she'd murdered John and Laura and run over Ken and tried to kill me. I thought she was going to shoot me, but she didn't. She pushed me into the basement, hit me on the head and locked the door. Did she think that nobody would find me?'

'Well, she set a fire in the sitting room,' Pete replied. 'If Ken hadn't woken up out of his coma when he did, the whole house could have been burned down.'

'With me in it!' Eve exclaimed. 'I feel sick. I could have been burnt to death!'

'It's all right, Eve. I'm here now,' David said gently. 'Come and sit down; you're shaking.' He paused, seeing the charred remains of Eve's sofa, then added, 'I'm afraid your sitting room's a bit of a mess.'

He knew Eve liked everything to look perfect and was surprised by her reply. 'It doesn't matter. At least I'm alive. I hated that sofa anyway.' She paused and looked around the room, disorientated. 'Where's Portia?' she asked. 'I need to give my dog a hug. That awful woman locked her outside.'

Pete went quiet, not knowing how to tell Eve.

'What is it? She hasn't killed my dog? Oh, please don't tell me she has!' Eve pleaded, almost in tears again.

'I'm sorry . . . Phyllis did poison the poor thing, but Annie's taken her to the vet in Chania so hopefully she'll be all right.'

Eve's tears started to fall again. 'It's all my fault if she dies.'

'No, it isn't, darling,' David soothed, holding her. 'Anyway, you know what a fighter Portia is; she'll be fine, I know she will.'

'I promise I'll never interfere like this

again,' Eve said earnestly, gazing up into David's anxious blue eyes.

David didn't truly believe her, but she was so beautiful and life was anything but boring with her. He decided she needed to be kissed again.

* * *

A little later the police arrived and Eve, impressed by their speed, conceded that they weren't as inefficient as she'd previously thought them to be. She was also surprised that they seemed genuinely concerned about what had happened. She had been worried they might tell her off for interfering again, but nobody mentioned her indiscretions.

A few minutes after the police turned up, Annie returned from Chania. Portia was still very ill, but the vet was doing everything he could to help her recover and she was putting up a good fight.

In all the excitement, Eve had forgotten that Phyllis had said she was going to the airport. As she started to recount the events of the evening to the police, Eve remembered the details of what Phyllis had said. Knowing that she had planned to get the last plane to Athens, Eve wondered what the time was. Would the police be too late — and would they be angry with her?

'Oh, no!' she cried. 'Please don't be cross with me, but with the fire and my dog and everything else, it went out of my mind! Phyllis told me she was heading for the airport and that she planned to catch the last plane to Athens this evening.'

'You should have told us this before,' the police inspector said. 'We might not get there in time.'

Eve was close to tears and turned to David. 'David, I really did forget. So much has happened and I really don't feel well.'

'Don't worry, darling,' he said, holding her close. 'If they don't pick her up in Chania, they'll be waiting in Athens. There's no way she'll escape.'

Eve wasn't reassured, believing Phyllis could still get away. She didn't think she'd feel safe until the police found her, and she was still tearful when Don walked in. Pete had phoned Don and Betty to tell them what had happened.

'Thank goodness you're safe, Eve,' Don exclaimed. 'What an awful experience to go through. I can hardly believe that Phyllis was capable of doing so many awful things. I just hope the police manage to catch her.'

'Phyllis told Eve she was getting a plane to Athens, so the police will get her either here or over there,' Pete said.

'How will she cope with jail, especially in a foreign country?' Annie asked. 'She barely speaks a word of Greek.'

'Well, that's her lookout,' Eve interjected. 'I'm sorry, but she tried to kill me and I don't care what happens to her! Though I expect it'll be hard on Betty . . . '

Eve felt a little guilty, knowing that Phyllis had been Betty's best friend.

'Yes,' Don replied. 'She's very upset. That's why she hasn't come with me. She's finding it all very hard to take in.'

Eve thought that probably wasn't the real reason, knowing that Betty would have to be nice to her after what she had been through and that would go against the grain. Her thoughts returned suddenly to being locked in the basement, and she imagined the fire taking hold and not being discovered. She burst into tears and David put his arms around her.

'It'll be all right,' he said gently. 'I'm here. I won't let anything like this happen to you again. Just promise me you won't go snooping around again in things that could be dangerous.'

'I won't — ever again!' Eve replied. 'I wouldn't want to have another experience like this again. And what about my dog? I'll never forgive myself if she doesn't pull through.'

'She's a strong girl,' David soothed. 'Just like her mistress.'

Annie smiled as she listened to their

quiet conversation. She thought that once Eve got over the shock, she wouldn't hesitate to get involved in things that didn't concern her, but as Annie watched them together she thought they made a perfect couple, even if she knew he would have his hands full — Eve was both unable and unwilling to live a quiet life!

When the police had left for the airport, Eve sank down on to a kitchen chair. 'Oh dear,' she said. 'I'm absolutely exhausted. This really has been some day. I think I could sleep for a week.'

'Come on, I'll take you upstairs,' David said.

Annie and Pete looked at each other and smiled.

20

The following day, Eve and David went to The Black Cat together, having arranged to meet Pete and Annie there for a celebratory drink.

Phyllis had been stopped just as she was getting on the plane for Athens the previous evening, and she was now in police custody. After a difficult night, Portia was now on the road to recovery, and so Eve felt life was just about perfect again.

As they walked into the bar, she was surprised to see Betty and Don sitting with Annie and Pete. It must have taken some courage for Betty to come and face Eve, knowing she would have to be pleasant and sympathetic.

For a moment Eve did feel sorry for her. After all, Phyllis had been her friend and it must have come as a huge shock to find out what she had done.

She imagined Betty would also be rather upset that Phyllis hadn't taken her into her confidence about her affair with John. Eve decided she would try and be nice to her, at least for today.

'Hi,' Eve said loudly to everyone. 'Drinks are on me today.'

Betty glared at her. Eve was showing off again.

'Betty,' Eve said gently. 'I'm so sorry that the murderer turned out to be Phyllis. I know she was a good friend of yours.'

'Not really,' Betty replied sharply. 'I just tried to help her when her husband died, but I never did get close to her. I certainly wouldn't call her my best friend.'

Betty wasn't going to show Eve that she was upset about Phyllis. She found it difficult to make friends, and now she felt as if she'd lost her only ally, not to mention how flattering it had been to have someone following her around doing whatever she asked. To top it all off, Betty had immediately noticed that

Eve and David were holding hands.

All her efforts to split them up had been pointless, and after all that Eve had been through, she knew she couldn't be nasty to her. However, she knew it would only be a matter of time before Eve began interfering in other people's business again, and she felt with grim satisfaction that David would soon get fed up with her.

Eve smiled and, as if she could read Betty's thoughts, took David in her arms. He was surprised at her open show of affection, but for once he didn't mind. He wanted everyone to know that Eve was his.

She looked into his eyes, remembering the previous night. Then, knowing that Betty was watching them, she forgot all her good intentions. She pulled David close and kissed him. To her delight he kissed her back with the same enthusiasm. Everybody in the bar clapped — except Betty, of course — and both Eve and David laughed delightedly.

There might have been three attempts on her life in as many weeks, but her short time on Crete had been filled with excitement, danger and love. Life couldn't be more perfect.

Eve Masters decided the best decision she had ever made had been to move to Greece.

But how long would it be before she needed again the excitement and adrenalin rush that the murders had given her? Would she be content with just looking forward to becoming Mrs David Baker — or would she need something else to spice up her life?

THE END

We do hope that you have enjoyed reading this large print book.

Did you know that all of our titles are available for purchase?

We publish a wide range of high quality large print books including:
Romances, Mysteries, Classics
General Fiction
Non Fiction and Westerns

Special interest titles available in large print are:
The Little Oxford Dictionary
Music Book, Song Book
Hymn Book, Service Book

Also available from us courtesy of Oxford University Press:
Young Readers' Dictionary
(large print edition)
Young Readers' Thesaurus
(large print edition)

For further information or a free brochure, please contact us at:
Ulverscroft Large Print Books Ltd.,
The Green, Bradgate Road, Anstey,
Leicester, LE7 7FU, England.
Tel: (00 44) 0116 236 4325
Fax: (00 44) 0116 234 0205

Other titles in the
Linford Romance Library:

SEEK NEW HORIZONS

Teresa Ashby

Sister Dominique, already having serious doubts about her calling, is sent on a mercy mission to South America after a devastating earthquake. There, she meets Dr Steve Daniels, and feelings she had never expected to experience again are stirred up. As she is thrown into caring for a relentless stream of casualties, her thoughts are in turmoil. How will she cope in the outside world if she leaves the sisterhood? And dare she allow herself to fall in love again?

HOUSE OF FEAR

Phyllis Mallett

Jill's twenty-first birthday is more than just a milestone — it marks the day her life changes forever . . . A letter arrives on the morning of her birthday; an invitation to travel to Crag House on the remote Scottish island of Inver to stay with the grandfather whose existence she had been completely unaware of. Whilst there, she meets her cousins, Owen and George, and handsome neighbour Robert Cameron. But her visit has involved her in a web of deceit that may threaten her life . . .

SUSPICIOUS HEART

Susan Udy

When Erin discovers that her mother's home and livelihood is under threat from the disturbingly handsome Sebastian, she knows she has to fight his plans every step of the way. However, she quickly realises Sebastian is equally determined to win, and he apparently has the backing of the entire village. When a campaign of intimidation is begun against Erin and her mother, it doesn't take her long to work out that it can only be Sebastian behind it . . .

THE RUNAWAYS

Patricia Robins

When Judith and Rocky elope to Gretna Green they sincerely believe marriage will solve all their problems. But the elopement proves to be the beginning of an entirely new set of difficulties ... Rocky begins to wonder if his parents were right — is he even in love? Were they too young after all? And in the background Gavin, Judith's boss, watches her disillusionment with a concern which is growing into something more ...

ANGEL'S TEARS

Teresa Ashby

Born in the same year that the Titanic sank, seventeen-year-old Cassandra Grant has the world at her feet. But tragedy strikes her family and Cassie has to grow up fast. She falls in love with Dr Michael Ryan — but then discovers he is about to be engaged to be married. Cassie leaves town to begin training as a midwife and tries to forget Michael, but tragedy strikes again and she has to return home where there are more surprises in store . . .